A WISP OF

Grace

CHRYSTAL J. GILKEY

Published by Embold Books

El Dorado, AR 71730

The story, all names, characters, and incidents portrayed in this production are fictitious. No identification with actual persons (living or deceased), places, buildings, and products is intended or should be inferred.

All scripture quotes are from the King James Bible Version

Identifiers:

LCCN: 2025922548

Paperback ISBN: 9798992045031

Hardcover ISBN: 9798992045048

Ebook ISBN: 9798992045024

Praise for A Wisp of Grace

Chrystal Gilkey provides a masterpiece of mystery, faith, and the subtle elegance of grace. *A Wisp of Grace* is both haunting and hopeful—a refreshing reminder that even in the darkest corners of the past, redemption endures and prevails. Readers who enjoy stories with spiritual depth and atmospheric intrigue will be mesmerized by this remarkable literary novel.

—Ian C. Griffin
Multiple Award Winning Author

I loved this story so much that I read it the entire thing in three hours. So much real life happens in this story but the elements of mystery and lurking strangers balanced the heavy life stuff. I love a happy ending and was totally rooting for Alice and Mark. How beautiful to see Mark's journey... I loved every minute of it. 5/5

—Savanna Loy
Author, Speaker

CHRYSTAL J. GILKEY

Series Information

Shady Springs Virtue Series

(In Order)

A Wisp of Faith

A Wisp of Hope

A Wisp of Grace

A Wisp of Mercy

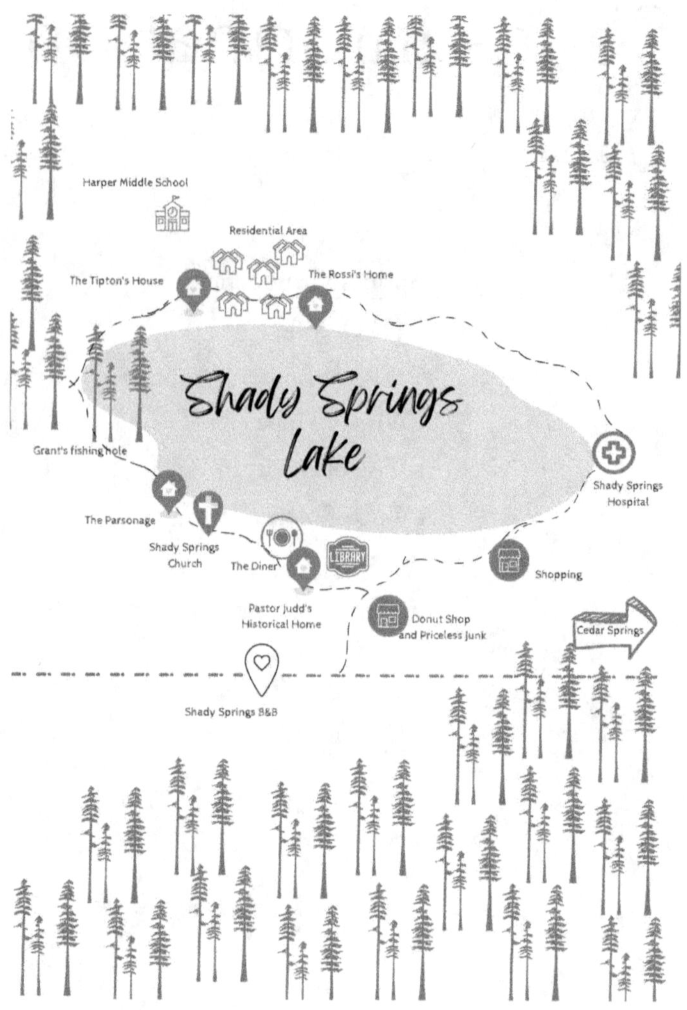

Harper Middle School
Residential Area
The Tipton's House
The Rossi's Home
Shady Springs
Lake
Grant's fishing hole
Shady Springs
Hospital
The Parsonage
Shady Springs
Church
The Diner
LIBRARY
Shopping
Pastor Judd's
Historical Home
Donut Shop
and Priceless Junk
Cedar Springs
Shady Springs B&B

To the people taking their second chances,
learning to receive grace,
as well as give grace to others.

CHAPTER 1

Alice

Looks like the perfect family.
—Alice

Rays of sunlight drifted through the attic window, high-lighting golden beams and particles floating in the air. To a child, it might have seemed magical; for Alice, it simply reminded her of her allergy to dust. A tingling, itchy sensation began to run down her arms. *Grant and Mercedes owe me big time for this. How did I ever let my brother talk me into spending my summer vacation before my senior year of college, covered in attic grime? He better pay me extra for my allergy medication!* Sighing at the thought, she pushed past boxes and piles of junk and made her way to the far corner of the attic. She tugged open an unlabeled box. Three options awaited the contents— donate, trash, or keep. A musty smell tickled her nose as she rifled through men's clothes. Shoving the outdated polyester back into the box, she scrawled "CLOTHES, DONATE" across the top with a black permanent marker.

An uneasy silence settled through the rafters as shadows from the setting sun emerged from attic corners. Alice shivered and fumbled for her favorite playlist on her phone. Soon, the room lightened with the happy, upbeat music. Smiling and humming one of her favorite songs, she grabbed a small box on an old chest.

"Aghh!" Alice screamed, throwing the box into the air. As it fell, tiny bits of paper and feathers rained like confetti. Something had renovated that little box into its home. "So gross!" Thank the Lord for the plastic gloves Mercedes had left for her. Shuddering, she picked up the box and dropped it into the large trash can. She grabbed her phone and texted her brother.

Better get a rodent exterminator, found a nest and droppings.

Great, he responded with a mouse face emoji.

I think I need extra compensation. You failed to mention you had rats!

Sorry, terms are nonnegotiable. Lol.

She slit the tape and slowly removed the lid of an unmarked box. *No rodents there.* She began to breathe easier. Manila file folders lay stacked nearly to the top, neatly labeled with Shady Springs Bank, 1971 tax statements, 1971 receipts, and so forth. She wrote "TRASH" on the top and shoved it into the waste pile. The following three boxes were large and heavy; she could barely scoot them from the attic wall. The boxes held bedding, pots and pans, silverware, and other random household items.

"Some of this is good stuff," Alice said aloud. *Who and why would anyone leave their silverware and blender behind? Did Grant and Mercedes need any of this?* she questioned inwardly. Shrugging her shoulders, she wrote across the boxes, "DONATE?" and slid the box to the side. Her brother and his new bride could go through them later.

Alice sighed and rolled her shoulders back. A blanket covered the following box. She lifted the corner edge and carefully slid the blanket onto the floor, not wanting the dust to invade her air space. She clapped her rubber-gloved hands in glee. "Oh, cool! A trunk!"

The blanket had done its job protecting the red wood grain. The chest appeared to be in good condition. Mercedes had told her if she wanted to keep anything from the attic, she could. Alice had always wanted a hope chest. She loved reading historical romance books and daydreaming about owning a trunk to hold cherished items for her future family home. *Would her father have made one for her if he was still alive?* The way her mother and brother talked about him, he seemed to be a jack-of-all-trades.

She wiped off the chest and pushed it open to reveal a photo album, quilt, and plastic crate. She pulled out the photo album and transported herself back to a time of dark-rimmed glasses, knee-length midi skirts, and muscle cars. Pictures of a smartly dressed man standing with his wife and daughter filled the album.

"Looks like the perfect family," she mused aloud to herself. *How can I throw someone's pictures away? If it was a previous pastor, the church or the historical society may want them.* She set the album in the donate pile. *Let someone else throw them away. I just can't.*

She carefully took the quilt out and admired it's vibrant fan pattern in hues of yellow and purple. One tiny stain blemished its left corner. She set it on top of the boxes with "DONATE?" for Mercedes to look at later.

The plastic crate contained another smaller rectangular object. Wood paneling encased the perimeter with something that looked like her childhood VHS tapes on the inside. Across the front in white letters, she read Phone-Mate Model 400 Automatic Telephone Answering Machine. It didn't look like any of the answering machines they had growing up. She remembered how her mom would get all three of them to record a family message before the beep sounded, signaling the end of the recording.

"Hello there. It's Carol, Grant, and Alice. You've reached the Ford family. Leave a message after the beep. You can't afford to wait." Her brother always said the corny line at the end, finding it hilarious. *I'll remember to tell Mercedes what a dork my brother was. Whatever happened to that old machine?* she wondered. As she took out the answering machine, a card slid out from underneath and fluttered to the ground. She carefully set the machine back in the box and picked up the card.

"To the pastor of Shady Springs," she began to read aloud. "I'm the sister to the pastor. I figure that's close enough." With a shrug of her shoulders, she began to open the note.

"Alice! Are you still here?" Mercedes called from the attic hatch.

"Yep! Still working!" She set the note on top of the machine and turned to greet her sister-in-law. As she did so, a movement reflected by the attic window caught her eye, and she moved closer to see. The window overlooked the backyard of the parsonage and a heavily forested area. Curious, she took a few steps toward the window. A dark figure holding binoculars stood by a tree and stared back at her.

She inhaled sharply and slid back against the wall out of sight. Closing her eyes, she tried to catch her breath. *What on earth?*

"Alice, are you all right? What are you doing against the wall?"

A hand touched her shoulder. Mercedes stood in front of her with a concerned expression.

"I saw something—someone— in the woods!" She could hear her voice tremble and hated how scared she felt. *Calm down. You're safe. Mercedes is with you,* she told herself.

Mercedes turned to the window and cautiously peered out.

"There's no one there, Alice. Are you sure you saw someone?"

"Yes. A man stood over there by the trees." Alice pointed in the direction in which she had seen the man.

"Okay, well, he's gone now. We'll let Grant know when he comes home. How about you take a break with me? Tea and cookies?"

Alice sniffed. Mercedes didn't believe her. She felt like a little kid. A tickle threatened under her nose, and she sneezed, causing them both to jump.

"Sorry." She laughed. "A break sounds great. And maybe another allergy pill."

They hurried down the pull-out ladder and downstairs to the living room.

"When's the last time they renovated this house?" Alice said.

"I'm not sure. Probably around the reign of green linoleum," Mercedes wrinkled her nose.

"At least there's no shag carpet," Alice joked.

"Yes. I'm also thankful someone painted the wall paneling at some point. The appliances work well, and the bathrooms are decent enough. No house payment, so that's a huge bonus," Mercedes added as she led her into the kitchen.

"How's married life? It's been what, six months?" Alice sat at the kitchen table while Mercedes put on the teakettle.

"Almost half a year—hard to believe. It's gone by fast with work and church but, I do love being married to your brother." Mercedes said with a twinkle in her eye.

"Okay, you can spare me the details. Please, stop there. Hearing you are happy is enough," Alice held up a hand.

"Very happy," Mercedes hesitated, fiddling with the tea strainers in their mugs. "I'm a little nervous about this Vacation Bible School meeting with the other ladies in the church Saturday night. I want to try some new ideas, but I'm unsure how the other ladies will respond." Steam rose from their mugs as she brought them to the table. Alice raised an eyebrow as her sister-in-law set the tea down, turned, and reached high on top of the refrigerator, pulling a package of cream-filled chocolate cookies from their hiding place.

Mercedes laughed at her questioning look. "You know how your brother is—anti-sugar and all that. If I buy sweets, there is always a lecture, so I hide them and eat them when he is not around," Mercedes smiled and shrugged. "Between you and me, I think he knows I have them but lets me have my little indulgences."

"Y'all are funny." Alice played with the strainer in her tea. "You shouldn't worry about the Vacation Bible School meeting. If you want some support, I'll come."

"That would be great. Sonja is coming as well. Maybe we can do some things differently with the three of us."

Alice took a sip of her tea and winced, burning her tongue. "How are things at work?"

"It's going well. My coworkers are behaving, and I get to do what I love." Mercedes twisted her cookie open and ate the cream part first.

"That one girl isn't giving you any more trouble?" Alice took a bite of her cookie, causing crumbs to fall onto the table.

"Kate? No, she's settled down. She's dating my boss Ryan, who she's been crushing on for years, so she's happy." Mercedes set her cookie ends on the table and reached for another.

"That's good." Alice watched her lick off the cream of another cookie in amusement. "Do you just eat the cream filling?"

Her sister-in-law colored slightly. "Am I a horrible person if I say yes?"

"Not at all. They are your cookies. Enjoy them how you like," Alice said.

"I don't feel as guilty about the sugar when I just eat the cream because I'm not eating the whole cookie," Mercedes confessed. "Did you get very far in the attic?"

"I think I made a dent. There are a few boxes I need you and Grant to look at." Alice tried another sip of her tea.

"Oooh, any treasure?" Mercedes stacked her cookie ends on the others and rested her elbows on the table.

"Depends on what you consider treasure. There are three large boxes with stuff randomly thrown in—silverware, a blender, and figurines. You might be able to use some of it. There is also a pretty cedar chest." Alice thought back on the chest's contents. "The chest contained a quilt and an old photo album. I set the quilt out for you. It was in good condition. The photo album I thought the historical society would want if it were a former preacher from Shady Springs."

"Good thinking!" Mercedes nodded her approval.

"Oh, there was also an old answering machine with a card addressed to the pastor of Shady Springs."

"What did the note say? Was the machine a gift?"

"Maybe, but I don't think so. The card hadn't been opened. I was about to open it when you came in, and I saw that creep." She shivered and rubbed her arms. "I know what I saw, Mercedes. There really was a guy there."

"I believe you," Mercedes reassured her.

"Thanks," Alice gave her a small smile, and they silently sipped their tea.

After a moment, Mercedes spoke with a mischievous twinkle in her eye. "Maybe we should leave the machine and card on the table as a prank for Grant. Like someone left it for him as a gift."

"Okay. I'll go up and get it." Alice rose to her feet and stretched. Dust particles drifted from her clothes. "Oops, sorry, looks like I'm leaving a trail of attic grime." She sneezed again.

"How about I go up to the attic, and you take your allergy pill?" Mercedes offered.

"Good idea." Alice nodded and sneezed again, fumbling with her purse to get her medication. Swallowing her pill, she grabbed another cookie and leaned back at the table to wait.

Mercedes skidded back into the room, slid the machine and card on the table, and made a beeline to the back door. After checking the deadbolt lock and pulling the kitchen curtains tight, she pressed her back against the wall.

Alice froze, alarmed at the behavior change. "What happened?"

"I saw the man exactly where you said! I couldn't see his face because of the binoculars, but he wore a long, tan overcoat. He's gone now." Mercedes took a deep breath. "I'm calling Grant."

CHAPTER 2

Grant

A strange call, a mysterious trespasser, and
a cryptic message all in one day—
what are the odds?
—Grant

G rant Ford sat at the desk in his office and double-checked his calendar for the next few months. Summer vacation had started, and most of his congregation would soon be leaving, each embarking on their relaxing getaway. For him, though, those three months included activity after activity. Youth camp, Vacation Bible School, and more youth activities popped up on his schedule. Parents wanted their kids occupied and out of trouble during the summer, and a few children needed an escape from their homelife. In anticipation of their summer schedule, Grant recommended that Derek Rossi lead the youth department until the deacon board decided on a youth pastor. Derek had proven to be faithful in their men's Bible study group. He and his wife Sonja had recently adopted a teen boy and baby girl. Grant and the board thought they would be great to work with the youth. The couple seemed ecstatic with their new role.

Grant felt a tingling in his toes as he scanned the summer calendar. His people were on fire, and he knew the Lord would do big things in the next few months. Sliding his calendar in his desk drawer, he grabbed his keys. Mercedes should be home now. *I wonder if Alice made any headway in the attic.* He chuckled at the thought of his sister sticking her hand in a rat den. The church had been packing stuff left behind by his predecessors and leaving it in the attic for years. He had finally gotten permission from the church elders to throw away whatever was up there.

He stood and started for the door when the church phone rang. He sighed and glanced at his watch. Two minutes after four o'clock. Technically, he was off duty. He could leave, let the message machine pick it up, and no one would be the wiser. The phone rang again as if it would not stand for being ignored.

Grant rolled his eyes and picked it up.

"Shady Springs Church, this is Pastor Grant." He paused, waiting for a response. Silence.

"Hello?" Still nothing, not even a breath. He started to hang up when he heard a faint sound. Curious, he brought it again to his ear. "Hello, is anyone there?"

"Do you help those in need?" a male voice replied on the other end.

"We try to help when we can. Do you need help?" Grant asked. He received many calls for money to help pay bills, put gas in cars, etc. Sometimes, the calls rang genuine, but many wanted cash for alcohol or drugs. He would often decline if they didn't let him pay the bill directly or go with them to put gas in their cars.

"Everyone needs help. Everyone needs grace. Do you give grace?" the voice persisted.

Oh boy, this person is a real nutjob. Grant rubbed his hand through his hair.

"I'm not sure exactly what you mean. Why don't you come by the church sometime, and we'll talk about how we can help you," Grant said.

"You will be tested," the voice said, ignoring Grant's invitation.

"All right then, have a good evening." Grant disconnected the call in frustration.

The strange conversation replayed in his head as he pulled into his driveway. *What did the man mean when he said tested?* Maybe it was time to get caller I.D. on the church line.

All thoughts vanished as his wife appeared in the doorway of their home. He took the steps two at a time and stopped abruptly at her furrowed eyes.

"What's wrong?" He wrapped his arms around her and kissed her on the cheek.

"Hurry, come inside, and I'll tell you," she said, pulling him into the entry hall and shutting the door.

"You didn't answer my phone call," Mercedes said.

"When did you call? I didn't hear it ring." Grant checked his phone—three missed calls. "I'm sorry, I must've been on my bike when you called. I can't hear anything when I ride."

"It's fine. You're here now." Mercedes led him into the kitchen.

"Hey, Sis." Grant took in his sister's pallor and held up his hands. "Okay, what's going on?"

"Someone was in the backyard," Mercedes began.

"With binoculars. A man!" Alice chimed in.

Grant crossed over to the kitchen window to look.

"He's not there now. He's gone—disappeared." Mercedes paced the kitchen.

"Why don't you have a seat, Mercedes? Then, start from the beginning." Grant tried to calm his wife so she could tell him what had happened.

"You start. You saw the man first." Mercedes sat by Alice and nudged her.

"Go ahead, Alice," he prompted, joining them at the table.

"I was working in the attic, and Mercedes came home. Something caught my attention in the attic window. When I checked it out, I saw a man standing by the trees."

"Who?" Grant asked.

"I don't know. His binoculars covered his face, and he wore a long trench coat."

"When I went to look, he had disappeared. Alice looked terrified," Mercedes said.

"I thought you said you saw him," Grant said, trying to put the pieces together.

"We came downstairs for a tea break. I went back to the attic to get something. When I rechecked the window, I saw a creepy man with binoculars. By the time I came downstairs, he had vanished, and I called you."

"Next time, just call the police," Grant's stomach churned at the thought someone was watching his house and, more importantly, his wife. "I'd feel much better if they came by, and it turned out to be nothing than if they didn't come and something were to happen. We should call them now so they can have it documented. Who knows, maybe a neighbor has also reported a suspicious character."

He dialed the number to the police department and confirmed a patrolman would be in their neighborhood in ten minutes.

"I'll feel safer knowing they've looked around," Mercedes said.

"For sure," Alice agreed.

"What is this?" Grant asked, gesturing at what appeared to be an old answering machine on his kitchen table.

"Oh, that," Mercedes hesitated.

"Did you find this in the attic?"

The girls glanced at each other and shrugged.

"We might as well tell him, Mercedes. We were going to prank you with it," Alice gave a little laugh.

"Prank me? How so?" He crossed his arms.

"The machine had a note made out to the Pastor of Shady Springs. We were going to leave it on the table, as if someone had left it for you as a gift," Alice explained.

"Then I saw the stranger outside, and he ruined it," Mercedes said flatly.

"Well, I don't mean to bust your bubble, but it will take much more than that to get me." Grant leaned against the counter and laughed at their expressions of annoyance.

"Famous last words. You better watch out now." Alice scrunched her nose up at him.

"Ooh, I'm so worried. How will I ever sleep tonight?" Grant winked at them and grabbed the card. Curious, he slid his finger through the edge to open it and pulled out a folded, yellow-lined paper. His jaw tightened as he read it.

"What is it? What does it say?" Mercedes asked.

"Yeah, read it aloud," Alice said.

He thought about lying and telling the girls it was nothing. They had already been through an ordeal tonight. *Crunch it into a ball and throw it in the trash can.* He shook his head and tried to act nonchalant.

"Basically gibberish, it says, 'Dear Pastor, I'm writing to inform you the pastor and congregation of Shady Springs have been tested every forty or so years. I refused to believe it when I took the pastorate. A letter was left for me by the previous shepherd, and I ridiculed it. I threw it away. That is why I must now write to warn you. You will be tested. Those closest to you will be tested. If you fail, the consequences are dire. I leave Shady

Springs humbled and shamed. You and your family must pass, or you will suffer the same fate I did. Be wary of those around you. If you don't believe me, listen to the recordings. People are never as they seem. — M.P.'"

"Creepy," Mercedes rubbed her arms.

"I agree. That note doesn't scare you at all?" Alice asked.

"It is creepy, but it has to be a hoax. I don't know. Maybe it's some sort of pastor initiation?" Grant said.

"A pastor initiation?" Mercedes snorted. "I've never heard of pastor hazing before. Let's listen to the recordings and see if they can shed some light on the matter." Mercedes pulled the answering machine toward her and studied the bottom of it. "We'll need four D batteries."

"I have some batteries in the garage. I'll go grab them." The strange call from his office replayed in his mind as Grant went to find the batteries. The caller had used those exact words: "You will be tested." He shook his head. There was no way they could be connected. The answering machine and note had been left in the attic, catching dust for who knows how long. What did the note say? *People are never as they seem.*

"Grant, the police are here," Mercedes called from the doorway.

"Oh, great. I'll be right there." He grabbed the batteries from his workbench and headed to the front of the house. For a moment, he had forgotten entirely about the peeping Tom. Grant didn't believe in coincidences. There was something else at work here. *A strange call, a mysterious trespasser, and a cryptic message all in one day—what are the odds?*

The following day, Grant rose early and began to make breakfast. The police had found no evidence of someone in his backyard, and their neighborhood search yielded nothing. After the police left, they tried to get the answering machine to play with no luck. Alice had suggested they take it to the pawn shop to see if they could get it to work. He smirked as he remembered how he had pestered his sister the night before.

"Didn't Mark Wildmen take over the shop after his dad passed?" Grant had asked. He loved to rile his sister.

"Yes, he did. And don't you dare start, Grant! Mark is quite good with machines. That's the only reason I thought of him." Alice crossed her arms and glowered at him.

"You sure are quick to deny any other motive," Mercedes said with a smile.

"Traitor! If you knew him like I did, y'all wouldn't be teasing me the way you are," Alice pouted.

"Well, go on and tell us then," Mercedes said.

"It's getting late. How about we continue this conversation tomorrow on the way to the pawn shop? I want to hear those tapes." Alice had stomped off, much to their amusement.

Grant flipped slices of bacon in the pan. It reminded him of all the tossing and turning he had done last night. Worrying for his wife and how to keep her safe, worry for himself and the test had plagued his sleep. Taking the bacon out, he cracked a few eggs in the pan. Mercedes liked her eggs scrambled with cheese and salsa. He would eat his eggs in any form as long as she was happy.

"Morning." He felt familiar arms slipping around him as his wife kissed him on the cheek. "Do I smell bacon and coffee?" She gave him a sleepy smile.

"That you do." He kissed her back.

"Ugh, do we have to start the morning this way?" a voice interrupted.

"For the rest of our lives." Grant winked at his sister and dipped his wife low, kissing her again.

Mercedes hit his arm and slid away.

"Grant, quit aggravating your sister. Sometimes you're impossible." Mercedes smacked his behind and grabbed a cup of coffee.

"Impossibly in love." Grant sang the opening lines to "When a Man Loves a Woman" into his spatula. He finished with a dramatic spin and bowed to his sister and wife. "Hold the applause. I'll be here all morning."

"Just ignore him." Mercedes grabbed Alice's elbow, and they escaped into the living room.

"That's right, don't mess with the cook," Grant called after them. He stared happily at his eggs and then, remembering their task for today, sobered immediately. He removed a plate from the cupboard and slid the eggs from the pan to the plate.

"Breakfast is ready. Come fix your plates!"

The girls came in giggling but stopped short as they reached the table with the answering machine and card.

"I sure hope Mark Wildmen can give us some answers with that machine." Grant broke the silence as he sat with his plate. They ate quickly, each eager to solve this mystery. On the way to the pawn shop, Grant couldn't help but take one last jab at his sister. *That's what older brothers do, right?*

"So, Alice, what exactly went on with you and Mark?" Grant studied his sister in the rearview mirror. She crossed her arms and glared at him.

"What? You said you would tell us on the way there," Grant said innocently.

"You did say you would tell us," Mercedes reminded her.

"Fine. It's not even that big of a deal. Mark was supposed to take me to our senior banquet but never showed up. Everyone said he dropped out of high school the next day." Alice sighed.

"He stood you up?" Mercedes asked.

"Yep. Until your wedding, I hadn't seen or heard from Mark Wildmen since. He tried to speak to me at your wedding, but I ignored him."

Alice looked out the window. Her sad expression made Grant feel like a heel for even bringing it up. Mercedes frowned at him.

"Sorry, we don't have to talk about him anymore if you don't want to," said Mercedes.

"It's okay. Like I said, it's not a big deal. I haven't thought about Mark in a long time, and I'm sure he still doesn't think about me."

Grant gripped the steering wheel. *How could a guy forget a sweetheart like his sister?* Alice told him once the boys her age at church were intimidated by him and were too afraid to ask her out. Secretly, he had been glad to hear that. Without a father to look out for her, his duty was to protect his sister. Mark better mind his p's and q's. Regardless of what his sister said, that guy had hurt her.

Like the other businesses in town, the pawn shop sat around the lake's perimeter. The founders of Shady Springs made the lake the focal point and built the city around it. They passed the church and library. A few blocks farther, they pulled into a small storefront, sandwiched between a donut shop and a nail salon. A wooden sign reading, *Priceless Junk,* hung in its window.

"Hey, maybe we should get our nails done while Grant talks about machinery with Mark?" Mercedes turned around excitedly. Grant tried not to roll his eyes.

"How about after I finish the attic?" Alice suggested. "I'd hate to mess them up on one of those old boxes."

"Sounds like a plan." Mercedes squealed and clapped her hands. Grant couldn't help but smile at her enthusiasm.

The girls exited the car and examined some of the "priceless junk." A few wicker chairs and an antique Tiffany floor lamp beside a bamboo table sat on display near the entrance.

Grant retrieved the answering machine and letter from the trunk of the car. As he neared the store's door, a voice called from behind.

"Excuse me, sir." He turned to see an elderly gentleman dressed in a threadbare jacket and faded shirt. A toe poked through the top of one of his shoes.

Curious, Grant handed the machine to Mercedes and asked her and Alice to take it inside. The old man seemed harmless enough, but one could never be too sure.

"Yes, can I help you?" Grant's reflection mirrored in the stranger's dark sunglasses.

"I seem to have left my wallet in my other pants. I ordered some donuts and coffee at the shop but cannot pay for them. Could you help me out?" The stranger cleared his throat and scratched the gray whiskers on his chin.

"Sure, let's go take care of it. I don't think I've seen you around Shady Springs before. Did you move here recently?" Grant stepped over to the door of the donut shop and held it open for the elderly gentleman.

"Here for a visit. Don't plan on staying long." The man led him to the counter and the teenage girl working there.

"He said he'll take care of my bill." The man pointed to Grant while Grant took out his wallet.

"How much is the bill?" Grant asked.

"Fifteen dollars." The teenager smacked her gum with a bored expression.

"Fifteen dollars? You must have been hungry." Grant smiled at the stranger.

"I was, but half of that was for the coffee. I don't know how coffee came to be so fancy or expensive. All it is is beans. Seven fifty for ground-up beans." The man grumbled and shook his head.

"I hear that," Grant agreed as he handed over some cash. "Well, you are all set now. My name is Grant Ford. I'm the pastor of Shady Springs. We'd love to have you come visit while you are in town."

"Thank you. I know who you are." The man turned and pushed open the door to leave.

"Wait, you didn't tell me your name," Grant persisted.

"Sure didn't. I'll be seeing you around." The man gave a small wave as he exited through the door.

Grant glanced back at the teenager, already transfixed by her phone. He rushed to the door to see which way the stranger left. The man had vanished without a donut crumb in sight.

CHAPTER 3

Mark

Could I ever be good enough for that someone?
— Mark

Mark felt his heart nearly drop to the floor when Alice Ford walked into his shop. The last time he spoke to Alice was at her brother's wedding. She hadn't given him the time of day.

"Hey, Alice, and uh, Mrs. Ford. What brings you ladies into my little shop?" Why on earth couldn't he remember that woman's name?

"You can call me Mercedes." Mercedes smiled at him, but her scrutinous gaze made him uneasy.

"How can I help you, ladies?" He said, trying to turn her focus away from him.

"Alice found an old answering machine in our attic. There are some messages on it, and we are curious to hear them. Grant tried to get it to work at home, but there seems to be something wrong with the machine." Mercedes set the machine down on a glass countertop covering an assortment of rings and watches.

"Cool, let's take a gander." Out of the corner of his eye, he could see Alice perusing the shop, looking everywhere but in his direction. *Nope, you are not going to ignore me today, honey.* He cleared his throat loudly to get her attention. "Wow, a PhoneMate answering machine. I think my grandma had one of these." He tried not to smile as Alice beelined to the counter.

"Are you familiar with them? Do you think we will get to listen to the recording?" Alice asked excitedly.

Mark stared into her deep blue eyes for a moment. A man could get lost in those eyes. He blinked and looked at the machine. "Yep. No problem."

"Great. When can you have it ready? It's kind of important." Alice sneezed.

"I'm sorry," Mercedes interjected. "My husband is supposed to be here. I'm not sure what is taking him so long. I'll be right back."

Alice watched her leave with a panicked expression.

It's because of me. She doesn't want to be left alone with me. Mark couldn't blame her. Although it had been some years ago, he hadn't left things all that great between them.

Alice sneezed again. "Geez, Mark. When's the last time you dusted in here?" Her eyes began to water.

He handed her a tissue. "Sorry, it's been a while. I've been taking inventory of things in the shop. It's been a slow process since my dad died."

"I heard about your father. I'm sorry," Alice rubbed her nose with the tissue.

"Thanks. We thought he had beaten it this time once the doctors gave the all-clear. It's crazy how fast the cancer spread, and then the old man refused the radiation treatment. He did half a treatment and told them never again," Mark crossed his arms.

"So, are you moving back to Shady Springs? What's your plan here?" Alice walked over to a hat display and tried on a large purple turban with a peacock feather. "What do you think?"

"My mom needs help with the shop, and my younger brother is still in college. That leaves me. We're still discussing what needs to happen. I hate to see the shop closed. It's like a piece of my dad. To him, these things were priceless. He loved going to estate sales and flea markets, finding the diamond in the rough." Mark crossed over to where she stood.

"I think this one is more your style." He plucked the purple monstrosity off her head and replaced it with a straw fedora. "Perfect for the summer and brings out your eyes."

He tucked a strand of her hair behind her ear. She jumped and stepped back, knocking down a cardboard stand-up of John Wayne.

"It takes a lot to bring down the Duke," he joked as he lifted the cutout from the floor. He couldn't help but notice the closer he moved toward her, the more she balked like a nervous filly.

A ring from the shop bell broke their conversation.

"We're back! Sorry it took so long," Mercedes said as she and Grant entered the shop.

"Nice hat, Sis," Grant said as he came over and shook Mark's hand. "Mark, how's it going? Did they tell you about the machine?"

Mark felt the applied pressure to his hand loud and clear. *Stay away from my sister*, it said.

"Sure did." He smiled back and met Grant's handshake with his own.

"When do you think you will have it ready?" Mercedes interrupted their little display of male ego.

Mark let go of Grant's hand and motioned back to the counter. "A few days?" Mark shrugged. "Shouldn't take too long."

"Mark said his grandma had the same machine." A hatless Alice spoke behind them.

"Really? What a coincidence," Grant said. Mark detected a hint of suspicion in his voice.

"They were pretty popular in the '70s. Y'all said this was important. Why do you think some old messages from the 1970s would be interesting?" Mark said.

"They had a weird note with them," Alice said.

"Alice," Grant warned.

"You might as well tell him," Alice said.

Grant sighed and pulled out the card. "This was the note found with the machine."

Mark opened the letter, wondering what all the fuss was about. As he read, he couldn't help but think of the many horror/stalker shows he'd seen.

"Totally unrelated, but equally as creepy—we've also had a stranger outside watching our house," Mercedes added.

"It all started yesterday," Alice said.

"You were there? Do you think the stranger was watching you specifically?" The thought of someone out there watching Alice made his skin crawl.

"I don't think it was me specifically. I mean, why would anyone be watching me?" Alice shrugged.

"It did start with you in the attic," Grant mused. "Maybe it's some psycho guy from your college?"

"I'm almost one-hundred-percent sure that is not what is happening," Alice rolled her eyes.

"I don't think we can rule out anything until we catch the guy if he returns," Grant said.

"I'll call you as soon as I fix this machine. Let me know if you find out who your mysterious watcher is," Mark said.

"We will. Thank you, Mark." Grant turned and led the way to the door with Mercedes in tow. Alice trailed behind and paused, turning around.

"It was good seeing you again, Mark." She gave him a small smile and left before he could respond.

Mark stood for a moment, stunned she had even spoken to him. He didn't deserve it, not with how he had left things between them. Of course, her being the bigger person was totally in line with who she was. He had been sweet on Alice Ford since junior high. The whole classroom tittered when his seventh-grade teacher paired them for an egg-baby project. Alice was an excellent student—him— not so much. Reading had always been difficult. He enjoyed it, but he read so slowly. To escape the embarrassment of reading aloud, he'd joke and distract the class with crazy antics. His teachers always chalked his poor work up to his wild behavior, not realizing he had an actual learning disability. How could he blame them? He turned the situation into a farce whenever he got called on or turned in his work.

The egg project was the first assignment he truly wanted to get right, for Alice's sake. Heck, even he felt sorry she had been paired up with a dimwit like himself.

"Mrs. Parker, do you think it's fair for a smart girl like Alice to partner with me? I mean, are you wantin' her to fail?" he called out after the teacher announced his name with hers.

"I think this will be an excellent opportunity for you to work with someone new. Who knows, maybe Alice can teach you something." The teacher moved on, but not before Mark heard her say under her breath, "Lord knows I haven't."

Unfortunately for Alice, Mark screwed up that project too. His younger brother Sammy was supposed to be babysitting the egg while Mark did his evening chores of mucking the horse stalls. Somehow, their egg baby got kidnapped by some rogue G.I. Joes, and when the army men moved to save the baby, the egg dropped onto the floor. He glued the pieces back together and apologized profusely to Alice. To his surprise, she laughed and laughed until she cried. "Our egg baby is Humpty Dumpty!"

Mark sighed and stared at the answering machine. Truth was, his grandmother never had an answering machine, and he had no clue how to get it working properly. Grant Ford saw through his story for sure. Geez, that guy made him nervous. *He knows you are no good. You don't stand a chance with Alice. Why do you get yourself into these situations?* He shook his head at himself and pulled out his laptop to see what he could find out about the make and model of the machine. A tiny jingle of the copper doorbell rang out.

"Be with you in a minute," he called. His dinosaur of a laptop warmed up with a low hum. He glanced around and saw an older man perusing the store. His screen finally stopped spinning, and he typed "answering machine repairs" into the search bar.

"Can I help you?" Leaving the dinosaur to do its searching, Mark peered closer at his customer. He surmised the man to be in his seventies, probably six foot tall in his prime, now hunched over to five foot ten.

"I'm just looking around," the man said, peering into the watch and jewelry cases. "You have nice stuff here."

"Thanks, family business. My dad's collection mostly."

"Used to have one of those machines," the man pointed at the PhoneMate.

"Really?" Mark couldn't hide the suspicion in his voice. What were the odds of a stranger with knowledge of this exact machine wandering in the same day he acquired it?

"Yes, back before we had these new-fangled devices. I can hardly get mine to work right." The man plopped a flip phone on the counter. Mark tried to suppress his reaction to the outdated cell phone.

"It might work better if you had a newer model. I don't think they make these anymore. May I?" He gestured to the phone.

The man shrugged and nodded as Mark picked up the phone.

"Yeah, I can see why you're having trouble with this. I have some newer cell phones I can bring out if you like?"

The man grunted something Mark thought might be a yes.

"Hang on, they are in the back," he called over his shoulder. He hoped the man was genuinely interested; he could really use the sale. His family owned the store building, so he didn't have a monthly rent or mortgage, but his mother needed sales from the store to supplement her income. Grabbing the case of phones, he hurried back to the front to see his customer lifting the answering machine and studying it.

"I'm sorry. That's not for sale. Someone brought it in for repair." He set the phones on the counter. "I think you'll find these very easy to use."

The man set the machine down. "There's a trick I used to do with mine back in the day. When the tape gets stuck, you flick the top like this." He flipped on the switch. Mark started to protest as the machine clicked to a stop, but then the man tapped twice on the plexiglass cover. The tape began to whir.

"You have three messages..." A robotic voice came through the speakers. The man winced and turned off the machine.

"Wow! Thank you! Do you still want to look at the phones?" Mark couldn't believe his luck.

The man stared at the machine and scratched at the stubble on his chin. He shook his head and backed out the aisle toward the door.

"No, no thanks." The man glanced back at the machine and hurried out the door.

Mark sighed and returned the phones to the back room to catalog later. He had started taking pictures and uploading items for an online store. His father had fought the internet for so long. Hank Wildmen would be rolling in his grave if he knew what his oldest son was up to.

Mark never imagined himself working at his father's shop. The look on his parents' faces when he told them he was dropping out of school still haunted him today. His dad had kicked him out, thinking it would force him back into school. *I was so wild back then. Lord only knows why I am the way I am. My mother and father loved me. Why did I constantly rebel against them?*

Instead of returning to school, he picked up work for a logging company. He thought he'd be living the high life. He found out quick there's not much to do in a small logging town. After work, he'd go to the bar with a few other men. He stared into their eyes, dimmed with regretful stories, and swore he wouldn't end up like them. *Why didn't I return to my dad and accept responsibility for my actions? That would have been more like Sammy.* Two years younger, Sammy was the baby of the family and got off with a lighter punishment for every antic they committed together. *I'll never forget my brother's pleading with me the day I packed my duffel bag and left for good.*

"Why, Mark? Why can't you try harder and stay? Please don't leave." His brother had begged.

He had hugged his brother tight. "I just can't. You know school's not for me. There has to be something better out there—something bigger for me. Don't be sad. I'll call, I promise."

Mark wiped a tear at the memory of the lie he had told. There had been no phone calls to his brother. His gaze drifted back to the wood-paneled box sitting on the counter. For him, it symbolized a new beginning and a reconnection with something, no, *someone* good.

Could I ever be good enough for that someone?

CHAPTER 4

Mercedes

How can the Lord use someone like me?
—Mercedes

"Okay, I've got to concentrate on this meeting." Mercedes sat at her dining room table, pulled out her notebook, and reorganized her printouts of Pinterest ideas for decorations, crafts, and snacks. She always loved helping with Vacation Bible School at her home church. As a teen, she had felt she contributed to something bigger than herself. Grant loved getting the youth involved and told her no matter what the other ladies said, he wanted the teenagers to have roles in the event.

"How's it coming?" Grant kissed her on the cheek and grabbed water from the fridge.

"Good. I think I'm ready. I'm excited to share these ideas." She smiled at her husband.

"You'll do great. I'm going out for a run. Call me if you need anything during the meeting or any reinforcement. I know how difficult a few of our ladies can be."

Mercedes agreed she would and began to gather her handouts together. After her first encounter with Gladys, one of the senior ladies at the church, Mercedes nearly walked out of Shady Springs for good. Gladys had insinuated she wasn't good enough for Grant or their church. Later, Gladys apologized, but the seeds of doubt had been planted, and they still wanted to spring back up. Mercedes loved the people at Shady Springs but felt intimidated by their spiritual maturity. The recent renewal of her relationship with the Lord caused her, at times, to feel like an impostor. *How can the Lord use someone like me? I know so little about being a pastor's wife.*

A call from Sonja broke through her thoughts.

"Hey, girl, want to ride together?" Sonja asked.

"Yes, that would be great." Mercedes stuck everything inside her binder.

"All right, see you in about five minutes!"

Riding with her friend would help get her out of her head and her thoughts. She said a quick prayer, "Lord, please be with us at our planning meeting. Help us accomplish what needs to be done. Keep in our hearts that this event is for You and to minister to our children. Use us to provide what they need. Let the ladies be open to new ideas and give me the confidence to speak to them."

The doorbell rang. "Amen." She grabbed her binder and swung open the door.

"You didn't have to get out of the—" She stopped and stared, startled at the stranger in front of her. He wore a navy sweatshirt and blue jeans.

"Hey there, I didn't mean to startle you. My car ran out of gas right in front of the gas station four blocks over, if you can believe it."

"Lucky you were at the station," Mercedes said, still startled by the man's appearance. *What does this guy want from me?*

"Anyway, I'm sorry to bug you. I left my credit card at home and don't normally carry cash. Everyone I've asked either didn't have money or just flat-out shut the door in my face." He shoved his hands in his pockets and looked at the ground.

"Oh, gosh. I'm not sure if I have any cash. Let me check with my husband. Hang on just a second." She closed the door behind her and called Grant.

"What's up?" Grant breathed hard into the phone.

"Sorry to interrupt your run, but a man is here asking for gas money. He says his car ran out of gas at the service station, and no one will help him. He left his credit card at home."

"Don't give him any cash. I just bought some gas gift cards for situations like this. You can give him one of those. It should be enough to get him where he needs to go. They are on the end table by the door. I was planning to take them to the church tomorrow. The guy lucked out. Keep me on the phone in case he tries anything."

Mercedes grabbed one of the gas cards and opened the door. "Here's a gas card that should help you get where you need to go." She handed it to him.

"Thank you so much. I was about to give up hope." The man smiled sadly.

"Hang on a second," Mercedes said, taking in his wearied demeanor. She ran to the fridge and grabbed a bottle of water and a church tract.

"Here, take a drink for the walk back and something to read on the way."

The man's eyes lit up as he took the bottle from her. "Thank you so much for your kindness," he said as she shut the door.

"Did you get the man's name?" Grant asked.

"Oh, no, I didn't think about it." She opened the door again to ask, but he had already left the porch. She walked down the sidewalk, but the man had vanished altogether. "I don't know where he went. He's not on the street that I can see."

"Okay, just get into the house and lock the door. I'll be there in a minute."

"It's okay, Grant. I don't think that man was a threat. Sonja will be here in a minute anyway to pick me up."

"He could have been the watcher, Mercedes. Please wait in the house and lock the door."

Mercedes agreed as a sense of uneasiness overcame her. She hadn't felt any bad vibes coming off the man, but with the reminder of their creeper, she couldn't help but peek through the window. Sonja's vehicle pulled into the driveway, and she quickly grabbed her things to meet Sonja.

"You don't know how glad I am to see you." Mercedes shoved her purse into the floorboard and slammed the car door.

"What's wrong?" Sonja asked.

She caught a glimpse of Daniel, Sonja's son, in the rearview mirror—no need to freak him out as well. "I'll tell you later. How's it going, Daniel? Are you going to help plan Vacation Bible School?"

Daniel shrugged his shoulders. "Might as well, got nothing better to do."

"He's grounded from his video games till he gets his math grade up," Sonja whispered.

"Daniel, I came up with a couple of new ideas. Would you take a look at them and tell me what you think? I could use a young person's opinion." Mercedes handed him her binder. She watched as he sighed and began to look through it.

"You made a binder?" Sonja said with a laugh.

"I couldn't help it. I love binders. They make me happy," Mercedes grinned back at her.

They pulled into the parking lot of Bluebonnets and Razorbacks, a local diner in Shady Springs. Darlene, one of the owners, met them at the door.

"Gladys and the other ladies are in the private room in the back. What would you like to drink?"

They gave her their drink orders and greeted the other women. Gladys was there, of course, with a few members of the flower committee. Mercedes counted about ten women in all. *Not a bad turnout for a small congregation*, she thought.

"Ladies, I think we are all here now. Let's get started so we can get to eatin'," Gladys announced as they all took a seat.

Mercedes sat between Gertie, the owner of the Shady Springs B&B, and her friend Sonja. She motioned for Alice and Carol, Grant's mother, to sit with them.

"First of all, we are all tickled pink to have some new people to help plan this year's VBS." Gladys gestured to Mercedes and Sonja and then continued her spiel. "This year's theme is Treasure Island. Gertie, you can do the snacks. The flower committee and I will make a banner for the auditorium. Mercedes and Sonja, you can do the crafts. Alice and Carol will take care of registration. I think that about covers it." Gladys clasped her hands and sat down.

Sonja gave an encouraging look to Mercedes. "Go on," she elbowed her.

"Thank you, Gladys." Mercedes stood. *Here goes nothing.* "I think your delegation is just what we need, and I would like to add a few more helpers to your list. Pastor Grant mentioned he would like to see the youth help with this year's Vacation Bible School. He thinks with their help, we can make this year's VBS even better. Here are a few ideas that could help with decorating the auditorium. I also found a few ideas for snacks and crafts. Daniel, would you pass these out, please?" She handed him the packets.

"I'm not sure about these decorations," Gladys frowned. "How are we going to make a giant ship?"

"You will be surprised how creative our youth are. We have a very talented bunch," Mercedes smiled at Gladys, hoping the older woman would catch some positive vibes.

"We usually keep it simple, so we don't mess up the auditorium too much. Are the young ones even willing to help?" Gladys wrinkled her nose.

"Seems like they always play more than work," another woman said with disapproval. The women began to titter about how much work the teens would actually contribute.

"Well, I think these snack ideas are cute, and I would love to work with some of the teens to make them, especially since Pastor Grant has requested it," Gertie said.

"Thank you, Gertie," Mercedes tried to hide her disappointment. Gladys pursed her lips, and Mercedes could tell she still wasn't convinced.

"I'll have a list of the youth who want to help tomorrow, and then you can decide which ones you want to help you," Sonja announced.

"Great," Mercedes said.

"Y'all about ready to order?" Darlene stood in the doorway of the room.

Mercedes gave Gladys a quizzical look.

"Yes, I think we are ready," Gladys muttered.

Hushed whispers from other tables caused Mercedes to question her decision to try and change anything. *Why would they listen to you in the first place? They've been doing this for years.*

"Don't worry about them. They'll come around," Alice said.

"Am I that obvious?" She felt like her face was on fire.

"Not so much. I know how you are. Don't doubt yourself," Alice winked at her.

"You know I've served under many different pastors and their wives over the years. There is always a little resistance to change. People get used to doing things a certain way, but there is always room for growth. You are doing just fine, dear," Gertie assured her.

"I thought the ship in the auditorium was pretty cool. I want to help make that," Daniel added.

"Daniel is exceptional at art, especially painting." Sonja flipped her silky black hair and smiled.

"Just not at math." He pulled his hoodie over his curly red top and looked down at his hands.

"Take your hood off at the table, Daniel," Sonja said.

He glared at his mom and then softened his gaze. "Yes, ma'am."

"You'll get it, Daniel. It just might take some extra work. I had a hard time in math, too," Mercedes empathized.

"Thanks. I see some friends from school. Can I talk to them real quick?" he pleaded to his mother.

"Sure." Sonja smiled as he left the table. "I worry about him being a loner at school. He's had so much happen to him this past year, with the death of both his parents, being kidnapped by his crazy aunt, and then adopted. I'm just glad he has made some friends."

"He's a great kid, and you are doing a great job with him," she said, gently squeezing her friend's elbow.

"Watch the plates, they're hot!" Darlene warned as she slid their plates across the table.

After everyone had their plate and started digging in, Sonja leaned over and said, "Can you tell me what happened while Daniel's busy?"

Mercedes filled her in on the strange man asking for gas money. "I guess it wouldn't have seemed so weird if I hadn't caught someone spying on us the other day."

"Wait, what is this about someone spying on you?" Sonja's eyebrows furrowed with concern.

"The other day, we caught a man in our backyard watching the house with binoculars. Alice and I both saw him. Grant called the police, but they never found him." Mercedes took a bite of her juicy burger and closed her eyes. She hadn't realized how hungry she was.

"Did you tell her about the answering machine and the strange note?" Alice asked.

Gertie set down her fork. Her eyes never left Alice as she retold the contents of the mysterious message.

"Was the note signed by the pastor who left it?" Gertie said.

"Just initials. I think they were MP," Mercedes said.

"MP? I don't recall a pastor from Shady Springs with those initials. Unless it was—" She stopped mid-sentence and closed her eyes. "Oh my. Oh no."

"What is it, Gertie? Do you know who he is?" Mercedes set her hamburger down and leaned forward.

"I've got to go. I need to find Chase." Gertie stood abruptly and made a beeline for the door.

"Wait, Gertie? Can you tell us what it's about?" Mercedes followed her.

Gertie shook her head without breaking stride. "If this is about who I think it is, the pastor is the least of our worries. I can't believe this is happening again. I don't have time to explain now. I have to find Chase."

Mercedes stood stunned as the woman hurried out of the restaurant in distress.

"What was all that about? I've never seen Gertie so flustered." Gladys stood next to her.

"I honestly have no idea," Mercedes pursed her lips. *If I give Gladys one inch of information, she will run with it for a mile. The last thing our church needs is more kindling for the rumor mill.*

CHAPTER 5

Alice

Don't fall for that act, Mom.
I've already learned the hard way.
—Alice

Alice awoke Sunday morning with butterflies in her stomach—something big was going to happen. She grabbed the new summer dress her mother had gotten her and wiggled into it. The hem hung a tad shorter than her other dresses. She hoped she didn't spend the day tugging the pale green print down. Cool air brushed against her skin in the back as she made her way from her room to the kitchen.

"Mom, are you sure about this dress?" She gave her mother a little turn for a 360 view.

"It's a little low in the back, but I think it is still modest. If the dress makes you uncomfortable, then don't wear it. It won't hurt my feelings." Carol sipped her coffee.

Alice, not having the time or energy to pick out something else, sighed and stood beside her mother at the table.

"Is that roast I smell?" she said, sniffing the air.

"Yes, Grant and Mercedes are coming over for Sunday lunch. I sure hope that creeper stays away from their house. I worry about you cleaning the attic while they are at work." Her mother squeezed her elbow.

"You and me both. There is still a lot to go through in their attic, but I have all summer. I could wait and work over there when they are off work." Alice grabbed some oats from the pantry and almond milk from the fridge. She poured both into a pot on the stove, stirring until the oats softened.

"I think that's a wise idea—at least, until they can sort this mess out." Her mother stood and hugged her. "Let me know when you finish eating, and we can leave for church."

"Why are you so fidgety?" Carol said. Alice shifted in her seat and stood up.

"I don't know. I feel antsy. I'm going to go outside before Sunday school starts. Maybe some fresh air will help." Alice walked out the door and stood on the white steps of the church. The morning air felt hot and sticky. She walked to the edge of the steps where she could catch a glimpse of the lake. A couple of geese frolicked at the water's edge.

"Well, ain't you looking pretty?" A familiar voice spoke behind her.

"Mark Wildmen. What are you doing here?" She turned in shock. *I don't think I've ever seen Mark in a church service.*

"I got the machine working, and I figured instead of calling your brother, I would stop by a service and see what all this is about." He motioned to the church building.

"You mean church?"

"Well, yeah. I mean, why not? I at least know you." Mark grinned at her. He had the dreamiest grin. The girls back in high school would melt at the sight of his dimples. *How many girls do you think he's charmed since high school?* The somber thought broke through his dimple spell. Annoyed with how fast she could succumb to his charms, she quickly turned away.

"You will let me sit with you, right? I mean, unless you're embarrassed by me."

Did she detect a hint of nervousness? She peeked back to read his expression. He smiled, but his eyes held a glint of worry.

"Of course, I'm not embarrassed by you." Shaking her head, she motioned for him to follow her inside. She gestured to a chair in the back where her mother sat. "Here's where we usually sit. Mom, do you remember Mark Wildmen?"

"Of course. It's good to see you, Mark. I'm so sorry about your father. He was a good man." Her mother slid over a chair to make room, and Alice took the seat next to her.

"Thank you, Mrs. Ford," Mark said, sitting.

"Please, call me Carol," her mother said, holding out her hand and smiling.

"Carol," Mark said as he reached over Alice and shook her mother's hand.

Alice sat frozen, suddenly aware of how close he was to her. He still wore the same cologne he wore in high school. She tried to focus on Gladys, who was taking prayer requests in the front. When Gladys finished, one of the elders of the church began the Bible lesson.

"Who is the guy doing the lesson?" he whispered in her ear.

"That's Harold. He is one of the deacons in the church. He's a good guy and a family friend." She scooted away from him, hoping she could concentrate better.

"What's wrong? Do I smell?"

Why does he have to notice every little thing I do?

"No, you smell fine. I'm just trying to concentrate on the lesson, you know." She handed Mark an extra Bible that had been left under the chair. "Here, we are in Ephesians."

She opened to the chapter and tried to focus on what Harold was teaching. Every now and then, she would glance at Mark curiously. Mark appeared to be listening and trying to find verses.

When the lesson was over, people began to mill about before the worship service started.

"I don't believe I've seen you here before. Is this your first time here?" Alice looked up to see Chase Westin grinning from ear to ear. She felt her face grow hot. Chase had been a deacon at Shady Springs since before she was born. She loved him like a grandfather. One of his favorite pastimes was getting her goat. She would never hear the end of this!

"It is my first time here, thank you." Mark shook Chase's hand.

"Don't see Alice come in here with too many fellows," Chase said.

"Well, to be fair, she didn't ask me. I surprised her." Mark winked at Chase.

"We grew up together but are not here together," Alice clarified.

"Oh, I see. Together but not together. That makes total sense. Well, it's good to have you, Mark. And when you are *together...*" Chase paused and emphasized the word. "Take care of this girl. She's a special one."

Alice rolled her eyes. She did not need anyone to take care of her.

Mark scratched his head as the elderly gentleman left them. "There's another service after this?"

"Yes. Didn't you know what you were getting into?" She laughed.

"Nope. No idea."

"Did y'all not go to church growing up?" Alice couldn't remember ever talking to him about faith.

"We sometimes went to a church in Cedar Ridge, like for Easter and Christmas. That's where my mother's family is all from. My dad worked shift work until he retired and opened the pawn shop. My brother started attending a church at his college. He told me I should try attending church. Maybe I wouldn't be such a loser." His face turned red, and he looked at his hands.

"Don't say that. You're not a loser, Mark." Alice studied him. She always believed he was smart—maybe not book smart, but intelligent and kind in other ways—ways that truly mattered in this world.

When she was in second grade, Robby Beardman tried to bully her on the playground. "You ain't got no daddy. That makes you a bastard," he had sneered.

"Well, you ain't got no brain, so that makes you a scarecrow," she said, clenching her fists.

"Think you're so smart, huh? You better take that back," he threatened. He had pulled back his fist as if ready to swing at her.

"Or what? Whatcha gonna do, Robby?" A voice spoke from the side.

"Teach her a lesson, that's what. Mind your own business, Mark," Robby said, taking a menacing step toward her.

"I'm not afraid of you. You're nothing but a big bully." Alice braced herself. *And I have a big brother who can take care of you later,* she'd thought to herself.

But then Mark stepped between her and Robby. "What do you want to hit a girl for? Seems like your daddy should have taught you not to hit girls."

"Don't be talkin' about my daddy. Not unless you want me to hit on you," Robby focused his rage on Mark.

"Go ahead, take a swing," Mark smirked.

Later that day, Alice saw Mark nursing his busted lip while sitting on a bench outside the principal's office.

"Sorry you got your lip busted. Why'd you jump in anyhow?" Alice sat beside him. She'd never forget the look of glee on his face.

"I overheard one of the teachers say if Robby got in one more fight, he would expel him for the rest of the year. Figured it would be worth it, not having to put up with him for the rest of the school year."

Alice smiled at the memory.

"What?" Mark asked.

"Remember how you got Robby Beardman expelled in grade school? That was pretty clever for a second grader," Alice said.

"I can't believe you remember that. Seems like ages ago."

Grant started the service off by welcoming everyone.

"Is it weird having your brother as your pastor?" Mark whispered.

"Not really. He can be annoying sometimes, but he has always been there for me. He's a pretty good brother." Alice glanced at him, and saw tears welling in his eyes.

"Are you okay?" She placed her hand on his arm.

"Yeah, I'm fine." He shrugged her hand off and crossed his arms.

As Grant began his sermon, Alice tried hard to listen. Mark made it nearly impossible. He kept squirming around and accidentally knocked the Bible off the chair.

"Sorry," he said.

"It's fine," she whispered. She almost felt sorry for him; he looked miserable.

When everyone stood for the invitation, Mark looked confused and leaned over. "What is everyone doing?" he said as a few people went to the platform and knelt in prayer.

"If you feel like God is speaking to you about something, then this is an opportunity to go and pray."

"The only thing speaking to me right now is my stomach," he joked. A couple sitting in the seat ahead of them turned around.

"Shh, it's almost over," Alice whispered.

"You are welcome to eat at our house for lunch, Mark," Carol said. Alice stared at her mother, mouth agape.

"That would be great, Carol. Thank you," Mark whispered back.

You are in so much trouble, Mom, Alice thought as she crossed her arms.

After the service, Mark left her to find Grant and tell him the news about his machine. "I'll see you at your house," he said, leaving her with a wink.

When he stood out of earshot, Alice turned to her mother. "What was that? Why did you invite him over for lunch?"

"Because it was the Christian thing to do. He looks like a lost puppy, Alice."

"Don't fall for that act, Mom." *I've already learned it the hard way.*

She huffed to the parking lot to pout and wait while her mom kept visiting. An older man in a navy windbreaker leaned against her mom's car.

"Excuse me, what are you doing?" A closer examination revealed a ripped jacket and scuffed-up shoes. Why was he even wearing a windbreaker in the summer? "This is my mother's car. I'm sorry you are going to have to move." She didn't mean to be rude, but with all the weird stuff going on, this guy gave her the creeps.

"Please, do you have any money or something to drink?" The man spoke in a raspy voice.

"No, I don't usually carry cash on me. You'll have to ask someone else." She scanned the parking lot. Not a soul in sight.

"You could ask my brother. He's the pastor—" She turned back to the man, only to find him gone. She whirled around, searching the parking lot for him.

"Who are you looking for?"

Alice jumped and then breathed a sigh of relief at the sight of her mother. "No one, let's go home." Her hands trembled as she opened the car door.

When they reached her house, she helped her mother get everything on the dining room table. Grant and Mercedes had started having Sunday lunch with her mom after they married. Typically, they would have her mom's melt-in-your-mouth roast and mashed potatoes with gravy. She set the last plate on the table as the doorbell rang.

"That must be Mark. Do you want me to get it, or do you want to?" Her mother winked at her.

"I still can't believe you invited him here," she said as she stomped to the door.

"If you'd rather me not be here, I can go." Mark leaned against the doorpost and gave her a pitiful expression.

"You are already here, Mark. Don't be silly." She grabbed his arm and pulled him into the foyer.

"Let me make myself clear," she whispered as she leaned closer so only he could hear.

"This is my turf, my home, and my family. I'm not the same wide-eyed girl I was in high school. I'm not interested in games. Don't mess with my family," she warned.

Mark leaned in closer, unaffected by her words. "I'm not here for games. I'm here for you."

His pointed words and the proximity of his lips were too much for her to handle. She stepped away as her mother met them in the hallway.

"Alice, I hope you are being hospitable to our guest. Why don't we sit in the living room until Mercedes and Grant arrive? Would you like some tea or water?"

"Tea would be great," he said as he sat down on the couch.

Alice wished she could wipe the smirk from his face.

"Will you fix him a glass, Alice? I've got to get out of these heels." Her mother disappeared down the hall, and Alice huffed to the kitchen.

When she returned to the living room with the tea, Mark stood staring at their family photographs on the wall.

"Thanks," he said as he took the glass from her. "Your brother looks a lot like your father."

"Yeah, I don't remember much about my dad. I was only five when he died," Alice said. "His face and mannerisms, his voice are all a blur now. I look at pictures of my family back then, and those people are foreign to me. We've all changed so much since he's been gone. My mother has always been an independent woman. She's had to be as a military wife. Packing up at a moment's notice, raising me and my brother, handling the finances... She told me once before my dad died, the thing that got her through was the hope of my dad returning. Once she knew he was never coming back, she learned to fully rely on God. My brother was angry for the longest time."

Her cell phone rang, interrupting the conversation. "It's Mercedes. Excuse me for a moment. ...Hey, Mercedes, are y'all on your way?" Alice's heart dropped as Mercedes explained their delay. "The police are going to check it out? Okay, no problem. We will see you soon." Alice set her phone on the end table and stared down at it.

"What is it? Did something happen?" Mark looked at her in concern.

"Hang on. Mom, come here for a minute," Alice called out.

"What is it?" Carol appeared barefoot in the doorway.

"The watcher is back. Grant saw him from the kitchen window this time, but when he went outside, the man vanished."

Carol covered her mouth in shock. "Did they call the police?"

"Yes, the police are on their way, but Grant doesn't think they will find anything. They didn't last time. Anyway, now they have to wait for the police to come. Mercedes said we should go ahead and start without them."

"Well, I'm glad they are both safe. Mark, you are probably starving. Come on into the kitchen and let's get some food in you." Carol motioned for them to follow her into the kitchen. "I don't want you at the parsonage alone anymore, Alice. Not until we find out what is going on." Carol cut off slabs of the roast beef and placed it on their plates as they sat at the table.

"Absolutely," Mark agreed. "We don't know what this guy's motives are."

Alice passed a bowl of mashed potatoes to Mark. "Did you listen at all to the recording on the tapes?"

"No, I didn't. I wanted to wait for you in case the tapes got messed up." He heaped a pile of buttery potatoes on his plate and passed the bowl to Carol.

She took the bowl and set it on the table. "I sure hope they can shed some light on what has happened here. I'm ready for things to return to normal."

CHAPTER 6

Grant

Three words, but they made no sense.
—Grant

Grant rose Monday morning, hoping they could get some answers. Mercedes already had coffee going. Her shift started early at the weather station. He liked to get up to see her before she left for work. Afterward, he would have his devotion and a morning run.

"I wish I could go with you and Alice to the store today to hear the recordings," Mercedes said.

"I'll record it on my phone when he plays it so you can hear it," Grant said.

"What did you think about Sunday lunch?" Mercedes poured some coffee into her travel mug.

"You mean with Mark?" Grant leaned against the counter.

Mercedes nodded.

"I don't know. I like the guy. I think he's a good person. Is he right for Alice? Time will tell. He's got to prove himself."

"I agree. I hope he can get it together, for Alice's sake. Call me on my lunch break and fill me in on everything. Be safe." Mercedes gave him a quick kiss goodbye.

"You too. Don't let your guard down. We don't know for sure where that creep is." Grant couldn't help but worry about her driving down those country roads alone. The police had found nothing in their search yesterday. *How can a person vanish into thin air?*

After his wife left, Grant sat at the dining table with his coffee and his Bible. His thoughts drifted back to their conversation regarding Mark Wildmen. He had a lot of charisma and charm—just a good, old country boy. But where did Mark stand spiritually? He'd looked like he wanted to bolt out the doors during the invitation. There was definite interest in his sister, which was a little concerning. He wanted his sister to be with a good Christian man.

God,

Please touch Mark Wildmen's life. I don't know if he has trusted You as his Savior, Lord; if he hasn't, I pray that he will. Place the right people in his life to show him Your way. Please help him to trust You and live a life for You. Be with Alice and give her wisdom. Help them both to trust their relationship with You. Be with Mercedes and me while all this crazy mess is going on. Give Mercedes confidence in working with our ladies. Keep my family safe, Lord. Place a hedge of protection around us and put

Your blessing over us. Help me lead our congregation in Your way, Lord, in paths of Your righteousness. Bless our church members. . .

He continued to pray as different church members, missionaries, and other people came to his mind. When he finished, he changed into shorts and tennis shoes for his morning run. He linked his earbuds to some worship music and began his route. The parsonage sat on about three acres. The previous pastor had created a few walking trails through the back. Grant loved to run them in the morning, just in time to catch the sunrise. Sweat started to drip down his neck. Mercedes said it was supposed to be in the nineties all week.

A campfire smell hit his nostrils as he turned a corner at the back end of the property. *I was so worried about Mercedes I didn't think about my safety. I've got no phone, no gun, and no way to get help.* He stopped and searched the area for smoke and quietly approached a hidden clearing from his running trail. His heart almost stopped at the sight of a green-and-gray two-person tent. Smoke tendrils arose from a makeshift firepit. A stick broke to the right of him. *Get back to the house!* Grant didn't waste any time. He sprinted back and called the police for the third time in four days.

Five minutes later, Grant greeted the officers at the door and led them toward the back of the property. "I know you are tired of hearing from me, but I couldn't believe it when I saw that tent. This guy has been staying on my property for who knows how long!" Grant led the officers back to the trail. "There it is," he pointed in the direction of the tarp. "I'll hang back here if you don't mind."

"You can go back to your house while we process the scene," an officer replied.

"Great. Thanks. I'm supposed to pick up my sister and run an errand. Do you need me to stick around?"

"No, you can go. We will call you if we have any more questions or to update you on what we find."

Grant returned to his house, changed clothes, and left to pick up his sister.

"You're not going to believe what happened this morning." He waited till Alice fastened her seat belt. "I found where the creeper has been hiding on our property."

"You're kidding? Where was he?"

"On the back corner of the property—"

"Wait, did you see the guy?" Alice interrupted.

"No, just where he's been staying." He looked over and saw Alice wrinkling her nose.

"It's so hot. Why would anybody want to camp out back there?"

"Beats me." He parked in front of the pawn shop. "Let's see if we can find some answers. By the way, what is going on with you and Mark? Anything I need to know about?" He raised an eyebrow half-jokingly, half-serious.

"Please don't start. We are just friends—at least on my end, anyway."

"You think he wants more?" Grant tried to mask the concern from his voice.

"I know he does. Don't worry. I'm not jumping into anything. Yesterday was his first time attending church except for an Easter or Christmas service. I don't think he's ever trusted the Lord as his Savior. I'm worried for him." Alice opened the car door.

"I'm praying for him. I could tell he was uncomfortable yesterday. Maybe this will be a turning point in his life. I think he is a good guy," Grant said as he exited the vehicle.

As they approached the building, Grant couldn't help but smile at the odd things Mark had put on the sidewalk for today—canoe paddles, a grandfather clock painted white with arms on its hips, and a wooden ship helm. He paused for a moment at the helm.

"Hey, we could use something like this for VBS." Grant snapped a picture and sent it to Mercedes.

"That would be cool!" Alice agreed as she opened the shop's door. The copper bell above the door clanged, announcing their arrival.

"Hey, guys, come on in!" Mark called out. "I've been photographing teaspoons for the last half hour. I've never been so happy to see someone." Mark crossed his eyes at them.

"What for?" Alice asked, picking up one of the spoons.

"Our online store. My dad always hated the idea, but I think it's the way to go if my mom wants to see any income from this place."

"Sounds like a great idea," Grant said.

"Thanks. Anyway, photographing and listing items has been slow going. I hope it's worth it in the end." Mark pulled out the answering machine from under the counter.

"Didn't seem to take you long to figure it out," Alice said.

Mark looked down and shrugged. "The day you dropped it off, a man came into the store and showed me a trick to get it working. He said he had one like it back in the day."

"That's a pretty strange coincidence. A guy coming in the very day we drop off the machine? Did he leave a name?" Grant asked.

"Strange, yes, and the dude was even stranger. He didn't leave a name. I'd never seen him before. He said he was from out of town." Mark set the machine on the table.

"Ready for me to play it?"

Grant pulled out his phone and opened the recording app. He nodded at Mark.

Mark switched the machine to play. When the machine started ticking, he flicked it twice, just like the man had done two days before. A computer-generated voice began to speak.

"You have three saved messages. First message. Friday, June 3rd, 1979."

A new voice sounded, "Pastor, you have been tested, and you failed. Your family was tested, and they failed. Judgment is coming. Heed this."

Beep. The voice on the machine cut off. A heavy sense of dread settled at the pit of Grant's stomach.

The automated voice came on again. "Second message. Saturday, June 4th, 1979."

"Pastor, grace is what was needed, and grace is where you failed. You have been given a second chance. You must succeed. You cannot run from this."

Beep.

"Run from what?" Alice whispered.

"Third message. Sunday, June 5th, 1979."

"Pastor, you have squandered your opportunities and must atone for your choices."

Beep.

The hairs on the back of Grant's neck stood on end. It was the same voice from his mysterious phone call. These messages were from forty years ago. How could the same person be calling him now, and why? None of this made any sense.

"Well, that was disturbing," Mark said.

"Extremely," Alice agreed.

"That's not the half of it. I got a call last Friday night saying I would be tested and asking if I helped others in need. I thought it was a prank, but it was the same voice as in those messages." Grant pointed at the machine.

"Wait, you got a phone call? On your cell phone?" Alice questioned.

"No, he called me at church. I'm sure it's the same guy."

"That seems improbable, seeing that these messages are decades old. Do you have the note you found with the machine?" Mark said.

Grant pulled the note out of his pocket and handed it to Mark to read.

"So basically, you will be tested, and the test will involve helping others? Is that it? That doesn't sound too hard." Mark passed the note to Alice, who read it to herself once more.

"I guess not. I mean, I usually help people unless I think they are trying to con me." Grant shrugged. He took the note from Alice, who had stood silent during the exchange. Her face looked ashen. "What's wrong? Aren't you feeling well?"

"I think I failed the test," Alice said softly.

"What do you mean?" Mark asked.

"Sunday, a man in the church parking lot was asking for money and water. He creeped me out, and I told him I didn't have any. Then it's like he just disappeared. I should've done something more for him. What if whoever came after M.P. comes after me now?"

"I'm sure you will be fine. We don't even know what happened to M.P. or his family. Let's not panic and jump to conclusions," Grant tried to assure her.

"We are not going to let anything happen to you," Mark said.

"We've got to find out what happened with M.P. and his family. Do you think Harold or Chase might know? Gertie said she was going to talk to Chase about it. In fact, she seemed upset when Mercedes mentioned M.P. to her, Alice said."

"Let me text them and see." Grant shot a message to Grumpy Old Men, his group chat that consisted of him and the two men.

The men loved to give each other a hard time, and Grant enjoyed their camaraderie immensely. "I guess we'll go home and wait."

"Do you want to take the machine home?" Mark said.

"Not really, but I guess we should. Thanks for all your help, Mark." Grant started to lift the machine from the counter when his phone rang.

"Hey, Harold, did you—"

"Chase is dead."

Grant tried to focus on Harold's words. Three words, but they made no sense. *Chase is dead?* Grant had just seen his friend yesterday. Chase had been as upbeat as ever. Sure, he had slowed down a bit this past year; but what he lacked in speed, he made up with spunk. *How had this happened? Why?*

"Grant, what is it? What's wrong?" Alice shook his arm.

"Do you need to sit down?" Mark asked.

He signaled for them to wait and turned his back to them. "I'm so sorry, Harold. I know this is more devastating for you than for anyone. He was your best friend. Let me try and wrap my head around this—" his voice cracked, and a sob escaped. "I'll call you later," he finished in a whisper. A kaleidoscope of memories of Chase from Grant's childhood to his recent wedding flooded his mind as tears began flowing down his cheeks.

"Grant. You're scaring me. What is it?" Alice whispered.

"Chase passed away last night, in his sleep. A peaceful way to go." He turned to his sister. Alice's face bunched up, and she began to cry.

"No, not yet! I still need him. Please, no," she whispered, shaking her head.

"I'm so sorry, Alice. I know how much he meant to you. He meant a lot to everyone. This is going to be difficult." Grant hugged his sister tight. "Mark, we will catch up with you later. I need to get Alice home, and I've got to get to the church. People are going to be calling and wanting information."

"Sure, no problem. Let me know if I can do anything to help," Mark said as Grant led his sobbing sister out of the store.

CHAPTER 7

Mark

It's hard to believe there can be peace for someone like me.
—Mark

The devastation and heartbreak on Alice's face nearly broke him. Memories of the loss of his father flashed through his mind. The fragility of life, the split-second change from happiness to sorrow, haunted him. Where was this peace others spoke of? It wasn't at the bar or in a lover's arms. They offered a short reprieve from life's pain but no long-term remedy. He sat in his chair with his elbows on his knees and his head in his hands. His brother's face came to mind. Mark felt proud of Sammy. He had his life on track, and there was something about him after his father's death that he couldn't quite put his finger on. *Maybe I could call him. Check on him.*

He pulled out his phone and pushed the recently added contact. He hadn't even had his brother's number before the funeral. *I've been so stupid, caught up in my own crap. Something could have happened to my brother, and I would have never known.*

Sammy answered, and the familiarity of his voice choked Mark.

"Are you all right, Mark?" Sammy said, concerned.

"Yes, I'm fine. I had some friends at the store, and they received bad news. It made me want to check on you. Silly, I guess." Mark picked up the teaspoons he had photographed and placed them back in their case.

"I'm glad you did call. I meant it when I said I wanted us to stay in touch."

"You have classes today?"

"Not till later tonight."

A long, awkward pause ensued, reminding Mark why he hated making phone calls. "Well, I just wanted to see how you are doing. I guess I don't have much to say."

"I'm fine. I'm trying to keep up with school and work. How are the shop and Mom?"

"The shop is slow. Mom seems to be doing well. Some days are better than others."

"I took a marketing class last semester. If you want, I could help you publish ads to drive traffic to the website."

Mark sighed a breath of relief. "Yeah, that would be great. I'm pretty much open to anything to get more business in here. I don't want to mess this up for Mom."

"You're doing fine, Mark. Mom told me how proud she is of you for handling everything."

"She did? Well, that's reassuring, I guess." He didn't know what to make of his mother and brother talking about him, but he supposed if it was a good thing, he didn't mind. "I went to church yesterday," he blurted out.

"Really?"

"You don't have to sound so shocked. Is it that hard to believe?"

"Well, kind of. I mean, you've never been interested in church before. What did you think?"

"I don't know. It seemed long. The class before the service was interesting. There were a couple of things that confused me." Mark pulled out a tray of earrings that he decided to upload next on the site.

"What confused you?"

"This person, Jesus. I don't understand why He would die for someone like me. My whole life, I haven't cared about anyone other than myself. I'm selfish, and I've done so many things I'm ashamed to admit. It's hard to believe there can be peace for someone like me."

"None of us deserve it, Mark. That's what grace is—getting something we don't deserve. Jesus died for you because He loves you. I didn't understand everything at first either, but after I took that first step of faith in believing in Him, things became easier to understand."

Mark forced a laugh. "I'm not like you, Sammy. I've done a lot of wrong. I don't deserve that kind of love."

"God thought you were worthy and, brother, I do too."

Mark heard a hitch in Sammy's voice. Was his brother crying? He felt a weight around him, pressing him to make a choice. He tried again to focus on his brother's voice.

"That's why He sent His Son Jesus. None of us are perfect, Mark. I still mess up, and if you choose Christ today, you'll still mess up tomorrow. The difference is you have Christ on your side to help you get back up."

A battle raged inside Mark, the fight between a choice of living with Christ or living with himself. *You don't have to decide now. You've got other things to worry about, like the shop,* a voice reasoned in his head.

"I guess I'm just not ready to make that choice." Mark felt a heavy pressure release him. He blinked, almost wanting to cry. With the pressure gone, he felt alone and empty. His brother's voice brought him back to reality.

"Don't wait too long to decide, Mark. If you want to discuss it, I'm here for you."

"Thanks, Sammy. I guess I'd better get back to the inventory." Mark sighed as he disconnected with his brother and took out a pair of earrings. He wrestled with trading his fun and wild lifestyle for something straitlaced and boring. *How much fun have you really been having?* a voice within argued. Annoyed with himself and his thinking, he put an old Elvis record on to silence his thoughts.

The doorbell rang just as he finished cataloging the last of the earrings. An older man in a windbreaker and a younger man in a sweatshirt approached the counter.

"Excuse me, I'm looking for a camera," the younger man spoke.

"Any camera in particular?" Mark asked. They had a few antique cameras and several newer models. Many people traded in their cameras for their cell phones.

"Just one that works and preferably not too expensive," the older man smiled, showing off his yellowed teeth.

"Let me pull a few off the shelf to show you. Are you fellows from around here?" Mark crossed to another part of the store and grabbed three cameras he thought might work for them.

"No, we are just visiting. We don't plan to stay in town long. My name is Gabe, and this is Mikey," the older man said.

"Glad to meet you. My name is Mark. This was my father's shop. He passed away a while back, and I've been running it for my mom." He laid the cameras on the counter for Mikey to look at.

"Your mother is blessed to have you." Gabe smiled at him.

"I think this camera will work." Mikey picked up a red digital camera in the lower price range.

"Great. I can give you a good deal on that one," Mark said.

"Do you think that maybe you could loan us the camera?" Mikey asked.

"Loan it?" Mark tried to hide his disappointment.

"Yeah, you see, I have a camera at home, but I wanted to take some pictures while we were on our trip. If you can loan me the camera, all I need to buy is the SD card. I hate to buy a camera when I already have one at home."

Mark wanted to kick them out of his store but controlled his impulse. "Tell you what, you got yourself a deal. Just fill out this paper with your contact information and bring me back the camera when you're finished with it."

The men looked at each other and then back at Mark with huge grins.

"Thank you, Mark, this means the world to me." Mikey grabbed a pen from the counter and filled out the form.

"You are a good man, Mark Wildmen," Gabe said.

"Um, thanks, I guess?" Mark watched the men curiously as they exited the shop. He looked down at the form Mikey had filled out.

Name: Mikey Angelo

Phone Number: 879-777-1234

"Mikey Angelo? Why do I feel like I've just been hoodwinked?" Mark smacked his forehead and hid the form under the register, not wanting to be reminded of his lapse of judgment.

CHAPTER 8

Mercedes

Now, will you please promise me you will not try and take down any more crazy people by yourself?
- Grant

Mercedes started the coffeepot and sat at the table to wait for the dark amber, miracle tonic. She tried to relieve the pressure on her forehead and under her eyes. Even though she had only known Chase for a year or two, his servant leadership and heart for the Lord touched her to her core. Grant had repeatedly mentioned how worn out Chase seemed to be getting. He never wanted to slow down. His body may have been in his eighties, but his mind was as sharp as ever. Her vision blurred, and she shook her head. *Don't start that crying again.*

The coffeepot gurgled. She stood to get a cup as her husband entered the kitchen. He walked a few steps to her before engulfing her in a tight hug. She wrapped her arms tightly around him.

"Morning." He held her for a minute longer before releasing her.

She pointed to a chair. "Have a seat. I'll fix you some coffee."

"Thanks. I had a hard time falling asleep." Grant took his cup from her as she joined him at the table.

"Yesterday was a lot to take in," Mercedes said.

"I think almost every person in town stopped by the church. Chase made quite an impact on our community. I have a feeling those who didn't get in touch yesterday will today."

"He was such a good man. I wish I had known him longer."

"Yeah, this will be a hard funeral to get through." Grant wiped away a few tears.

"Let me know when they decide on a date and time so I can take off work."

"Will do. Be careful going to work. Call me when you get there. They still haven't caught that guy," Grant reminded her.

"What did the messages say yesterday?"

"I completely forgot to tell you about them. I'm sorry. Basically, M.P. and his family failed the test and judgment was coming."

"Ominous." Mercedes rubbed her arms.

"Very. Alice seemed freaked out about them. She said she had already failed a test."

"How so?"

"Something about a man in the parking lot asking for money and water, and she had nothing to give him. She's terrified something is coming for her."

"I'll give her a call." Mercedes grabbed her purse and keys, pausing long enough to give her husband a kiss on the cheek before she went out the door. "I'll be praying for you today. Text me if you need me," she called over her shoulder.

As she got into her car, the sun began peering through the thick green foliage. The morning drive made her fall in love with God's creation more. On more than one occasion, she'd managed to see a few owls scouring the landscape for one last snack before the sun fully rose.

Rounding a curve, she noticed a tan sedan in her rearview mirror with a man behind the steering wheel. She drove farther down the road. At each turn, the car followed. Suspicious, she pulled into a gas station on the right side of the road. *Let's sit here a minute and see what he does.* Moments later, the sedan entered the station parking lot. The car drove past her and a couple people standing outside the station and then parked on the opposite side of the store. Mercedes held her breath to see if anyone exited the vehicle. No one. The driver appeared to be just sitting there.

Her hands balled into fists. *I should feel safe driving to work. I should feel secure in my home.* This man, whoever he was, had taken that from her. Mercedes took a deep breath. *This needs to end here and now.* She stepped out of her car and approached the rear of the sedan. The man's gray, expressionless eyes locked with hers in the reflection of the side mirror. The vehicle reversed, and she stumbled back.

"Wait! What do you want from us!" Mercedes called out. She tried to grab the door handle, but he pressed the gas and squealed out of the parking lot. *What just happened?* The people at the gas station gawked at her. She ducked her head and headed back to her vehicle.

"You did what?" Grant yelled.

Mercedes calmly relayed—for the third time—what had transpired on her way to work.

"Why on earth did you get out of the car? People get kidnapped from gas stations all the time."

"I'm tired of being afraid. I'm tired of looking over my shoulder all the time. I thought if I confronted him, we could at least find out what he wanted." She understood his frustration with her but wasn't sorry for her actions. "I got his license plate number, Grant. You can call Lydia at the police station and see what she can find out."

Lydia worked as one of the station dispatchers and happened to be a Shady Springs parishioner.

"Fine. Give me the number."

Mercedes winced at his tense tone. *He's just lost one of his closest mentors and friends. Give him some slack,* she reminded herself. She read him the number.

"I got it. Now, will you please promise me you won't try to take down any more crazy people by yourself?"

"Can you define take down?" Mercedes said.

"Mercedes."

She smiled at the exasperation in his voice. "Okay, I promise."

After they disconnected, Mercedes began her daily duties at the weather station and started another pot of coffee. Her coworker, Katie, would have a conniption if the coffee wasn't warm and ready by the start of her shift. The day passed quietly until Grant called right before she headed home.

"They got the guy," he said breathlessly.

"What? That was fast!" Mercedes held the phone with her shoulder as she wrestled her car keys out of her purse.

"They found him through the license plate number. The police pulled him over, and he's at the station now."

Mercedes dropped the keys and bent down to pick them up. "Did he say why he was watching us? Will they let us talk to him?"

"Lydia said he will only talk to you and me. Think you can meet me at the station?"

"Absolutely. I'm ready to get this behind us." She finally got the car door open and threw her stuff in.

When she reached the station, Grant stood at the front desk talking to Lydia.

"Are you okay?" He looked Mercedes over and hugged her tightly.

"Yes, I'm fine. Let's get some answers. Where is he?" She looked to Lydia for direction.

"Follow me. He's back here. So you know, he's not in handcuffs or anything. We have nothing to charge him with unless you want to press charges for trespassing."

Mercedes could feel her husband's shoulders tense. She lightly touched his arm. "Stay calm."

Lydia held a blue door open to what Mercedes supposed was their interrogation room. "Mercedes, Grant, this is Martin Pitrones. The man who has been trespassing on your property."

Mercedes couldn't quite reconcile the hunched-over elderly man at the table with the person who had tormented them the past few days. And yet, his gray, expressionless eyes now met hers with an echo of sadness.

"Martin Pitrones? Are you the M.P. who pastored Shady Springs all those years ago?" Grant asked.

The man nodded. They stood in uncomfortable silence, waiting for the man to speak, but he sat staring into space.

"So you are the same M.P. who left a note and answering machine in the parsonage?" Mercedes clarified.

"Yes. That's me. I had to warn whoever might be next for the testing."

"Have you been sleeping in our backyard? In the woods?" Mercedes studied the man's dark circles and the stubble on his chin.

"I was afraid people would recognize me. I knew Gertie at the B&B would for sure. She and Chase were close friends of mine." Martin rubbed his head.

"Have you heard about Chase?" Grant asked.

"No. What happened?" Martin said.

"Chase passed away Sunday night."

"I'm too late. They got to him." Martin brought his hands to his face.

"What do you mean they got to him?" Grant asked.

"Please sit." Martin gestured to the chairs in front of him.

Grant pulled a chair out for Mercedes, and they sat down.

"Will you please tell us what is going on? Why have you been watching our house, and what is with the cryptic messages on the answering machine?" Grant asked.

"To understand, we have to start back at the beginning, before you and I, back to when the town originally started. The pastor before me left a note, a note that had been passed down from pastor to pastor. I made the foolish decision to throw it away. The note said the congregation of Shady Springs could either be a blessing or a curse. When the founding pastor's wife died in the late 1800s, and her murderer committed suicide, Shady Springs entered a testing period. Every forty or so years, the town is tested. If her citizens pass their tests, they will receive a blessing. It could be a healing or something of monetary value. However, if her citizens fail their tests, they will be cursed. Families could be torn apart, sickness and even death might follow."

"This was all in a note?" Grant asked.

"Yes. I already told you that. Listen carefully!" The man banged on the table in frustration, causing Mercedes to jump.

This guy is one jump away from the deep end, she thought to herself.

"I think we've heard enough." Grant put his arm around her. They started to stand.

"Wait, please. I'm sorry, I get carried away. Let me at least tell you what happened to me. Maybe it will prevent you from losing your family."

The man hid his hands in his lap, his eyes pleading with them. Grant gave her a questioning look, and she nodded slightly. They still didn't have the answers they needed. They sat down, and he began his story.

CHAPTER 9

Martin

He that giveth unto the poor shall not lack: but he that hideth his eyes shall have many a curse.
—Proverbs 28:27(KJV)

"As a pastor, I aimed for perfection and settled for nothing less. My wife and children knew my expectations and performed their roles diligently. My congregation respected my authority and leadership. Never once had the deacons and trustees questioned my role or my decisions. The day started like any other day. Shower at six thirty. Dressed by 7:00. Newspaper arrived at 7:05. Coffee and breakfast finished by 7:30. I strolled out the door to pick up the morning paper at the same time I always did. I remember I was particularly excited that morning. The church board had a meeting later that day, and I had a new initiative. Some of the children colored pictures during my sermons. The mothers complained of their unruly behavior at home. If mothers made their children listen to me, the man of

God, they might behave better. All I had to do was merely mention it to my men, and the word would spread. 'Pastor Pitrones wants people of all ages to learn and pay attention. Coloring is a distraction. Children should be listening.' Looking back now, I was high on power and a complete idiot."

He took a sip of his drink and continued.

"Anyway, I picked up my paper and turned to go back into my house. A man appeared out of nowhere. No one else was on the street that early. He stood tall, about my height—nothing too remarkable about him. His scuffed brown shoes and threadbare coat indicated he couldn't be important to me. Another man stepped out from behind him. This man was a tad shorter and wore a patched-up suit jacket. He asked me if I showed grace. I felt indignant. Who was this man that I should answer to him? I told him I would call the police if they returned. This was a respectable neighborhood. We would not tolerate vagrants. I'll never forget the man's eyes. They flashed, and I thought maybe he was on drugs or alcohol. Now I think it was something supernatural."

"Supernatural?" Mercedes laughed.

"Yes. Laugh if you want, but normal happenstance cannot explain what happened next."

"So, what happened?" Grant leaned forward.

"They left. I continued with my day, except nothing went as planned. I went to the board meeting. The deacons called my new initiative petty. They said I was too strict and needed to relax. People were leaving the church because of me. I walked out in a huff. Then, I began receiving the calls—usually, a man asking for money. Tired of saying no, I stopped answering the phone. Then came the messages. Gertie and Chase received them, too."

"Wait, how were Gertie and Chase involved?" Mercedes said.

"Chase served as my assistant pastor and Gertie, the church secretary."

"I never knew either one served in those roles," Grant said.

"I wasn't an easy pastor to work with. I demanded to have a secretary and an assistant. The board placated me. It's embarrassing, looking back to see how I was back then." He shook his head and picked at his nails.

"On two separate occasions, strangers came into the church, and Gertie helped them—at least, that's what she told me. Chase, on the other hand, was extremely protective of the church. He thought these strangers were up to no good and kindly sent them on their way."

"I can't picture Chase not helping someone in need," Grant said.

"I'm not exactly sure what happened in his situation. Gertie would be able to tell you more. Remember, I'm the self-centered preacher in this story." Martin grimaced and stood, stretching his legs. Refusing to meet anyone's gaze, he turned toward the wall, continuing with his story.

"I didn't notice if others needed help and certainly didn't offer to give any assistance. The following day, I came home and found my wife with another man. Just like that, they ruined my life—family, pastorate, everything. I had failed my test. I packed the tapes and the answering machine, placed them in the attic, and left. I left my wife and her lover to pack the rest."

"So, what made you come back? And why all the spying and secrets?" Mercedes said.

"What was I supposed to say? Supernatural people come to this town every forty years and wreak havoc. Would you have believed me?" He slumped back to his chair but didn't sit down.

"No, probably not. Do you really believe they are supernatural?" Grant scooted his chair back.

"Yes, I do. I don't know if they are angels or demons. Who knows? Maybe they are aliens. I wanted to come and see for myself if they returned. I wanted to ensure you found the answering machine and listened to those messages," Martin said.

"Have you seen the men you saw all those years ago?" Mercedes said thoughtfully.

"I've seen one of them outside the pawnshop and the church—they have the same exact looks, clothes, and everything. I think they can change their looks, though, if needed. They usually travel in pairs and are men. I've been researching them." Martin could tell he had Mercedes' attention.

"You mean there have been other sightings of them?" she asked.

"Yes." He pulled a small notebook from his front pocket. "Similar sightings have been reported in towns like Santa Fe, Fort Worth, and Boston. I've even spoken to a pastor in Edinburgh who has had an angelic encounter. This has become my life's work."

"Has anyone taken pictures of them or gotten them to admit anything?" Mercedes said.

"No, once people realize they are more than human, they move on to another town. I've tried to take a few shots of them in town, but so far, I have been unsuccessful."

"Why did you say they got to Chase? Do you think they had something to do with his death?"

Martin sat down. "I told Chase and Gertie about the letter and everything before I left. Neither one believed me. Soon after though, Chase's wife discovered she couldn't bear children. I always wondered if the curse followed him all these years."

"It's true Chase and his wife couldn't have children, but I hardly believe they cursed him. Chase lived a full, blessed life. He didn't let the circumstance of not having children get in the way of his joy." Grant stood from the table. "I understand your concern over what happened all those years ago, but I don't want you in my backyard, following my wife, or calling me again. I think it's time you left Shady Springs."

"I've never called you, Grant. If you've gotten any weird calls, it's from them. It's started again," Martin said, rubbing his palms on his pants. "Do you think you've passed the test?"

Mercedes cast a worried look to Grant. "What if someone we know thinks they've failed? You had several chances. Do you think this person will get another chance?"

"I would advise that person to leave town."

Alice loaded another box of goods from the parsonage into her sporty red four-door. When Grant called her and told her the police had the man watching them in custody, she felt it safe enough to work at the parsonage. Her piles had gotten quite large and had become hard to maneuver around in the attic. She sent Mark a message.

Would you mind if I dropped a few things off at your shop for Grant and Mercedes? They want to donate them rather than sell them.

That would be great. I'll keep the shop open until you come. Mark replied instantly.

As she pulled in front of his shop, she honked twice.

"Arghh, what treasure do ye have for me today?" Mark said in a pirate voice.

"A little bit of everything, kind sir." Alice curtsied.

"Kind sir? Can't you tell I'm a ferocious pirate?" Mark pretended to take offense as he grabbed a box to carry in.

Alice laughed. She couldn't help it; his pirate voice sounded like a Muppet. He set the box on the floor by the counter. When they finished carrying in the boxes, he opened the top box.

"Silverware, nice. Oh boy. What do we have here? I think my mom had these curtains at her house growing up." He pulled out the polyester material sporting bright yellow and orange flowers on a dark green background.

"Very *Brady Bunch*," Alice smiled.

"So, they caught the creeper watching your brother and his wife?" He lowered the curtain back in the box and sat down on the counter, his gaze never leaving her face.

"Yeah, it looks that way. They are talking to him now at the police station. I hope they can get some answers." She hesitated, unsure what to do or say. She had dropped off the boxes and couldn't think of a reason to stay longer. Mark didn't look in a hurry to close his shop. "What did you think about church?" she asked.

"You know what I just realized. I haven't eaten yet. Have you? How 'bout I tell you over some dinner?" Mark pushed himself off the counter and crossed in front of her.

"I would have to follow you to the diner to make sure you show up. I wouldn't want to be stood up again like at our senior banquet." Alice looked at him coolly. *I promised myself I would not fall fast for you again. I intend to keep that promise.* Her back stiffened at the inward resolve.

"We can't let that go after all this time?" Mark said.

"I waited at the lake pier for half an hour. Everyone at school knew you were my date, and everyone knew when I showed up alone that Mark Wildmen stood me up." Alice crossed her arms and stared pointedly at him.

"Technically, I didn't stand you up," Mark crossed his arms, flexing his broad muscles.

"What are you talking about?"

"I showed up. I was there."

"Mark, how can you even—"

"I was a bit late. I'll admit to that. I forgot the darn corsage and had to go back to get it. When I returned, you were standing in the moonlight on the pier, looking pretty as a primrose."

"I don't believe it. You're lying."

"The silver moon was no competition for you in your silver gown."

"Well, why did you leave then?" She couldn't believe her ears after all these years.

"I was a coward. I didn't believe I could ever deserve someone like you." His admission left her speechless. "Now, how about allowing me to make it up to you with dinner? Please, Alice?"

Just say no, say no, Alice! her mind cautioned.

"Yes, I mean, fine," she relented as all her sensibility went out the window.

"Great, let me turn off the lights in the back. You might want to wait by the front door. It's hard to see with the shop lights off." He disappeared into a back room as Alice walked to the front.

What in the world are you doing? "I have no idea," she said aloud.

"What was that?" Mark appeared behind her, causing her to jump. "Sorry, didn't mean to startle you. I thought you said something to me." He opened the door for her.

"No, I wasn't talking to you. It's not important. I'll drive my car to the diner and meet you there."

"Sounds good." He whistled a happy tune as he strolled to his car.

She got in her car and followed him out of the shopping center's parking lot, stopping before she needed to turn. She checked the left for oncoming traffic. A man's face loomed at her through the window. She screamed.

"Do you have any money?" he yelled, banging on her window.

Get out of here, now! a voice insisted.

She shook her head frantically and pulled onto the road. By the time she reached the diner, she was sobbing.

"Alice, what's wrong?" Mark met her at her car in concern.

"A man showed up at my car asking for money. He yelled at me and scared me. I got away as fast as I could. What if that was another test and I failed? What am I going to do?"

Mark wrapped his arms around her, and she rested her head on his chest.

"Why is this happening to me? It's not fair."

"It's going to be okay, Alice. Your brother is getting answers from that guy right now. No one is going to let anything bad happen to you. You don't even know if that man was part of the test. He could have been some random stranger."

"I don't think this test is fair. How can I tell the difference between someone in need and a crazy psychopath killer?" She sniffed and stepped back from him.

"You did the right thing. You were alone, and it was getting dark. Let's go inside and get something to eat. Maybe Grant will call with some news."

"Did you know I received my first D when I had to partner with you back in junior high?" Alice said as she plunged her fry in mayonnaise, followed by a dip in the mustard.

"You never received a D until junior high? More importantly, why are you ruining a perfectly good fry?" Mark wrinkled his nose.

"Mustard and mayo are the best combination. And it's true, not a D until I worked with you."

For a split second, a flash of sadness crossed his face. He reached across the table and touched her hand, causing her to catch her breath.

"I'm sorry for that. I was a real knucklehead then," Mark said softly. Alice felt every muscle in her body freeze as he leaned in. "Got some of that perfect combination on your chin." His thumb brushed against her jaw and then he brought his thumb to his lips. "You know, that ain't half bad."

She sat stunned, reeling from his touch and teasing blue eyes. Clenching her napkin, she rubbed the spot where he had been so brazen. *Don't let him see he got to you.*

"How is the cataloging going?" She changed the subject.

"Slow. Of course, thanks to your brother, I'm even more behind now that I've acquired more treasure. It's too bad I don't know anyone home from college for the summer who could help me." He took a huge bite of his burger.

"Wow. If you had tried harder, you might have been able to get the whole thing in your mouth," she said sarcastically.

"If I were eating alone, I would have. I've saved my manners just for you. What about the other? Do you know of anyone who could help me?" He winked at her.

She rolled her eyes. "I'm pretty busy helping Grant with his attic. I don't know when I'll finish. Speaking of my brother." She held her phone so Mark could see *Grant* scroll across the screen. She answered the phone and put it on speakerphone so they could both listen.

"Hey, Grant, I'm with Mark at the diner, you're on speaker."

"We just finished talking with Martin Pitrones. It turns out the creeper and the former pastor of Shady Springs who left the answering machine are one and the same."

"Okay." Alice thought fast. "So, what happened to M.P. or Martin or whatever? He failed the tests, right? What was the consequence?"

"He lost his job and his family. But, Alice, he wasn't a good person, very self-righteous, very selfish. He said Chase failed the test. The result was that he couldn't have children, but I have a hard time believing that."

"Grant, I think I failed another test tonight. What's going to happen to me?"

"Alice, you are one of the most caring people I know—"

"Did you ask him? If we fail the test, what should we do?"

Grant sighed. "He said you should leave town, but, Alice, running away isn't the answer. I promise we are going to get to the bottom of this."

"Did he say who is behind all of it?" Mark interjected.

"He thinks they are supernatural beings, angels or demons. He's been tracking them to different locations across the world."

Alice stared at the phone, her heart sinking. "How are y'all going to do anything against an angel or demon?" she said in disbelief.

"That's just what he thinks, Sis. We will take everything he says with a grain of salt, okay? Mercedes and I are pulling into the driveway. We'll talk more tomorrow."

"Wait, have you received the arrangements for Chase's funeral yet?"

"Not yet. We should know more in the morning. I'll give you a call as soon as I know."

"All right. Love you."

"Love you too, Sis."

CHAPTER 10

Alice

God is not out to ruin your life.
—Carol

"Why are you awake so early? It's five in the morning." Her mom kissed Alice on the forehead.

"I couldn't sleep. Grant said the former pastor thought these strangers were supernatural. I decided to do an internet search for supernatural tests or visitors. Martin Pitrones said they destroyed his life. I'm terrified they are going to come after me next."

"Oh, Alice, you have a good heart and love the Lord. God is not out to ruin your life. He loves you." Carol wrapped her arm around Alice and hugged her tightly.

"I've been reading these articles about entertaining angels unaware. Mom, there are reports worldwide of these strangers helping people. I found an online post from a monk in Russia. He shared how he saw a homeless person on the sidewalk and wanted to avoid him by crossing the street. His friend disagreed and wanted to give the homeless person money. When the homeless man looked up at them, his eyes were crystal blue, filled with wisdom and holiness. His friend told him they had been tested. The homeless man was an angel."

"Alice, it's the internet. How can you take anything on it seriously?" her mother protested.

"If it's from multiple sources, there must be something to it. Abraham and Sarah entertained angels in the Bible, and the Lord sent angels into towns to see if any people still lived righteously." Alice stood and stretched her arms over her head. "I made some coffee. Would you like a cup?" she called over her shoulder as she walked into the kitchen.

"Yes, thank you. I don't want you obsessing over this. The Bible does say we need to be hospitable to those in need. However, God gives us discernment and intuition to be wary of those in pretense or who would do us harm. I still don't think you did anything wrong." Her mom sipped her coffee and leaned back in her chair. "What are your plans for the day?"

"Since we now know who the watcher is, I plan to return to the parsonage and continue working in the attic. I might have to take a few more boxes to Mark," Alice said. She also had another plan in her head, but she knew her mother would never approve.

"How are things going with Mark? We didn't get a chance to talk much when you came home last night."

"Complicated. I like him. He makes me laugh, and there is a vulnerability in him that makes me want to help him. He wants a relationship with me, but I don't want to get hurt. I can't tell if he's ready to settle down. The biggest issue is I'm unsure where he stands with the Lord. His coming to church was a big deal. If I shut him out, would that push him away from God?"

"Be patient. There's no rush. It's wise to wait to see how his relationship with God will go."

Alice nodded and took another sip of her coffee. When her mother left her to get ready for work, she searched online for a map of Shady Springs and sent it to their home printer. *There's gotta be a connection to the places we've seen these strange men.* She put an X on the donut shop where Grant had met a homeless guy and another on the parsonage where Mercedes had seen the man whose car broke down. Then she placed two more X's at the church and the street corner where she had her encounters. As she studied the map, she noticed another location in line with the others. A chill ran down her spine. If you connected the X's, they formed a straight line through a historical landmark, the old house of the founding pastor Judd Hart. She set the map on the table. She knew exactly where her first stop of the day would be.

Forty-five minutes later, she pulled onto a red dirt road leading to a cabin. Pastor Judd Hart founded the town of Shady Springs in the 1800s, in the midst of a cholera epidemic. He and a few survivors left their homes to build a new town untouched by the dreaded disease. Pastor Hart's journals testify that the Lord led the pastor and his congregation to their new residence by a cloud that remained in Shady Springs until almost a year ago.

The Historical Society maintained the property and house. Alice remembered touring the home with her class on a field trip. They had traveled to several different log cabins throughout the state. She parked in the empty parking lot next to the cabin. As she got out of the car, she couldn't help but notice the stillness. No chirping of birds or croaking of frogs, not even the annoying buzzing of a mosquito. The air stood still. It was unnerving. *Brilliant move, coming here alone, Alice. Great thinking.*

Beads of sweat accumulated around her brow as she approached the porch of the saddlebag log cabin. Two front doors and two windows graced the entrance of the Hart family home. Treading lightly up the wooden steps, she peered into the window of the first room. Many of the furnishings were original Hart family heirlooms. A table and chairs stood by a wood stove on the left. A small bed nestled near the far back wall, with a two-sided fireplace center right. Nothing looked disturbed. She tiptoed to the other window. The second room reflected a mirror image of the first, minus the table and stove. Her gaze wandered to the bed. She covered her mouth to silence a scream. Two vacant eyes stared back at her. A man, sprawled across the bed, stared at her unmoving. *Was he dead?* Time stood still. She held her breath. He blinked.

She screamed and scrambled across the porch and back down the steps, unsure which sounded louder—the thudding of her heart or her feet smacking across the wooden planks.

She ran behind her car and fumbled through her purse for her phone. She pressed the last call she had made, which happened to be Mark.

"Mark, there's a man here," she gasped, trying to catch her breath.

"What are you talking about? Where are you, and what man?"

Alice crouched behind her car and waited for the man to appear around the corner. "I'm at Pastor Judd Hart's family homestead. It's a long story. I thought the homestead might be connected to our visitors and the testing and came to investigate. There didn't appear to be anyone here, but then I found a man in the cabin."

"Well, what did he say? Did he do anything?"

"He blinked." She shuddered.

"He blinked?" Mark sounded confused.

"I seriously thought he was dead! His eyes were empty, and then he blinked. Scared the crap out of me, so I ran."

"Did he chase after you?"

"I don't think so. I would be able to hear him walking across those creaking floorboards. I'm hiding behind my car right now." She kept her gaze fixated on the old place in case he made his move.

"Look, I'm heading out there right now, but you need to get in your car and call the cops. The guy is trespassing, at the very least. Let them handle it. Do not go back to the cabin."

Relief flooded over Alice as she recognized the dispatcher's voice as Lydia. She quickly explained the situation.

"I've got officers heading your direction right now. Have you seen the man come out of the cabin?" Lydia asked.

"No, that's weird, right?" A thought crossed her mind. "Lydia, what if he needed help? Like he was sick or something and couldn't get up?"

"A patrolman should be there soon, and they will check it out. You stay out of sight and on the line until they get there."

"I've already failed two tests," she said under her breath.

"What?" Lydia asked.

"Nothing. I, um, it's nothing." Alice stood and crept to the side of the house. With her phone gripped tightly to her ear, she peered around the corner. Nothing there. There was no sign of the man, and both front doors remained tightly closed. She leaned her head against the side of the cabin. *What now?* She heard a soft groan.

"Help, please help."

Alice closed her eyes and tried to think. He needed help. What if the policeman arrived too late? Could she live with herself if he died because she was too cowardly to act? She grabbed a can of pepper spray from her purse. Grant's college gift to her was finally going to come in handy. She breathed out slowly and started up the steps.

"Hello? Are you all right?" she yelled out.

"Who are you talking to, Alice? Do not go back into the cabin!"

She turned the volume down on her phone.

"A copperhead bit me. I don't think I'm going to make it much longer," the man weakly replied.

"Help is on the way. Why are you out here all by yourself?" She moved along the porch to the room the man occupied and glanced through the window. He hadn't moved at all.

"I'm visiting from out of town. I'm a photographer. I got a little lost, and then, well, the copperhead found me."

Alice saw a red camera sitting on the table. The story seemed to make sense.

"The police are just a few minutes away. I'm coming in through the door. Don't try anything funny." She went to the door and cautiously entered the room.

"You don't have to worry about me. I read once that limiting your movement keeps the venom from spreading quickly. Also, I have some numbness in the leg where he bit me."

"Where are you from? Do you have a family to call?" Alice moved in close enough to see his face better but far enough to remain out of reach.

"I have a friend who I travel with. He sure would have a time with this story. Snakes and us, well, let's say there's a bit of history there." He chuckled and then winced.

"Do you want me to call him? Do you have a phone?" Her radar went up again as she waited for his answer. Nobody went without a cell phone.

"Batteries dead. You don't trust easily, do you?" He studied her carefully.

"Too many bad things happen to girls who are on their own. Makes it hard to trust and hard to help sometimes."

He closed his eyes. "That is wise, Alice. Listen to your gut; it will guide you to who needs you."

Red-and-blue lights flashed through the window. "Help is here. I'm going to go out to meet them, so they don't do something crazy—like shoot you."

She heard him chuckle as she left the room.

"I'm Officer Traynor. You are in so much trouble with Lydia right now. The ambulance is on its way." Officer Traynor pushed past her and through the door. "Is the vic in the other room?"

"What are you talking about? He's lying right there on the bed?" Alice pushed past her into the room. The bed sat empty, the covers unwrinkled.

"He was right there. Look, there's his camera." She pointed to the camera sitting on the table by the bed. Officer Traynor pulled her gun from her holster.

"Stay behind me," she ordered as she approached the closed door leading to the other room.

She swung open the door and glanced inside, "No one's here."

"Where's the guy?" A voice spoke from the front entryway.

"Mark!" Alice ran without thinking and let him pull her into a protective embrace.

"Did you see anyone outside when you pulled in?" Officer Traynor asked, gun still ready.

"No, ma'am. No one," Mark said, shaking his head.

"I'm going to check the perimeter. You two stay inside the cabin. Try and follow directions this time." She gave Alice a pointed look.

"What was that about?" Mark asked.

"No clue." Alice shrugged her shoulders and walked back into the other bedroom.

"Really?" Mark said, following her.

"The guy said a copperhead had bitten him. He could barely move. How could he get out of here so fast without anyone seeing him?"

"Are you sure he was injured?"

"I don't know. He seemed like he was really in pain. Why would anyone fake an injury like that? And he left his camera behind."

"That's his camera?" Mark asked.

"Yeah, why?"

"I loaned this camera to a fellow who came in the other day. He left some bogus information, and I was sure I'd been conned." Mark picked the camera up incredulously and tried to turn it on.

"Drats. It needs charging. Maybe the pictures on here will give us a clue to who we are dealing with."

"Or *what* we are dealing with," Alice said.

"I'll be taking that," a voice spoke behind them. They turned to face Officer Traynor holding open an evidence bag. Mark dropped the camera in.

"Can you please let us know what you find on it?" Alice said.

"Girl, you're supposed to be asking for forgiveness, not favors." The cop turned on her heel.

"Officer, what she means is we'd really be interested in knowing what's on that camera. I recognize that camera from my shop—well, actually—my dad's shop. You see, he died recently."

Alice inwardly rolled her eyes as Mark made the most pitiful expression. *Like that's going to work.*

The officer's gaze softened. "Of course, I'll see what I can do."

"Thank you, Officer Traynor." Mark winked at Alice behind the woman's back.

CHAPTER 11

Grant

At first, I wanted to be a better man for Alice, but I realized I needed to be better for myself.
—Mark

Grant stared at the same passage of scripture he had already read three times that morning. He couldn't focus on anything—Martin Pitrones and his wild story, Alice's crazy antics yesterday, and the death of one of his dearest friends. He sighed and tried reading the passage in Ephesians Chapter 2 again.

But God, who is rich in mercy, for his great love wherewith he loved us,

even when we were dead in sins, hath quickened us together with Christ, (by grace ye are saved;) and hath raised us up together, and made us sit together in heavenly places in Christ Jesus:

that in the ages to come he might shew the exceeding riches of his grace in his kindness toward us through Christ Jesus.

For by grace are ye saved through faith; and that not of your-
selves: it is the gift of God:

not of works, lest any man should boast.

"Thank you, Lord, for your grace—for your gift of salvation through your Son, Jesus. I know any good in me is from you alone, Lord. Help me and my congregation share your grace and kindness to others. Revive our hearts and turn us again to you, Lord."

"Pastor Grant, is this a bad time?" Gertie poked her head through his office door.

"Not at all, Gertie. It's never a bad time to visit with you. Have a seat." He stood to greet her.

"I've been trying out new recipes. These are my summer strawberry scones. I thought you and Mercedes could be my guinea pigs. Well, at least Mercedes. I know you don't indulge in sweets much," Gertie said.

"Thank you, Gertie, that's thoughtful of you. Mercedes will be most grateful. Don't tell her I told you this, but I keep finding sweets stashed around our house. She buys them but doesn't want me to know about them. At least she can eat these in the open." Grant laughed as he took the plate from her.

"Leave the poor girl alone about her sweets, Grant. A little sugar now and then never hurt anyone."

"I can tell I am not going to win this argument." He held his hands up in surrender. "How can I serve you today?"

"I wanted to check on the arrangements for Chase's funeral. Have they decided on a time or place yet?" Her voice cracked, and she grabbed a tissue from his desk. "Sorry, his death was so sudden. I wish I had gotten to say goodbye."

"It's going to be hard for a while. I keep waiting for him to pop in the door and ask me to give him something else to do. He was involved in so many ministries." Grant grabbed a tissue himself and wiped his eyes. "His brother did call about his funeral. They scheduled the viewing for Friday night and the funeral for Saturday. Did you know he was in the Navy? He'll have the military funeral honors at the graveside."

Gertie nodded. "He would have liked that."

"You know, speaking of Chase. I never knew he served as assistant pastor at Shady Springs back in the day, or that you were the church secretary."

Gertie's face paled. "That happened years ago. Who told you?"

"Did you hear about the watcher at our house?"

Gertie nodded in response.

"Turns out it was the former pastor, Martin Pitrones. He told us about the testing." Grant leaned forward. "I got to know, Gertie, what your take is. Martin said Chase failed the test all those years ago and even suggested it as a cause of his death."

Gertie shook her head. "That man. When I heard these be-ings, whom I thought were angels, were back in our town, I reached out to Chase. He said not to worry about it because of your heart for people. He also said the person he spoke to all those years ago was not one of the angels. That person wanted money for drugs and ended up robbing and killing a man."

"I knew it. I knew Chase wouldn't have failed. How did you know the person who came to ask you for money was sincere?"

"I was sitting in the foyer at a little help desk Martin had made up. He made life around here miserable, let me tell you. I've never seen a more prideful, self-righteous man. Anyway, I only worked at the church three days a week, Tuesday through Thursday. On Thursday, a man came in whistling the tune of "Amazing Grace." His shirt was missing a couple of buttons, and his toes poked out of his shoes. He stopped at my little table and asked if the church could help him. He'd lost his job and needed twenty-five dollars to pay his water bill. I told him the church didn't have funds for things like that. His eyes were different. I don't know how to describe it, discerning, maybe. It was like he weighed everything I said."

"So, what happened next? I thought you ended up giving him the money?" Grant scratched his head.

"I did. I went with my gut. I felt his genuineness. Martin would never have agreed to give him any money from the church, so I gave him some of my own. And that's not all." Gertie smiled. "Two days later, I received a check in the mail for fifty dollars, two times what I gave the man."

"That's amazing, Gertie. You can never outgive the Lord, can you?" Grant said thoughtfully.

"Nope. Sure can't."

As Mercedes quickly changed out of her work clothes and into her church clothes, her mind drifted back to the VBS meeting earlier in the week. She hadn't felt peace with the way she left things with Gladys. Gladys had overseen their VBS for years and probably felt railroaded. *I should have talked to her beforehand. I got so excited about everything. It would have gone a long way if I had just front-loaded this information to her beforehand.*

"I think I should apologize to Gladys," Mercedes told her husband as she got in the truck.

"Why is that?" Grant gave her a puzzled look.

"If I had talked to her about the changes I wanted to make with Vacation Bible School before the meeting, maybe things wouldn't have been so awkward."

Grant shrugged, "Maybe, but honestly, I wanted those changes to happen as well. It's not about who is in charge or calling the shots but what is best for our congregation and people. Bringing the youth on board and working alongside the older members is a good thing."

"Even so, I feel like I need to speak to her," Mercedes said. When they reached the church parking lot, Gladys stood at the door waiting.

"Looks like she wants to speak to you as well." Grant raised an eyebrow and laughed.

"Here goes nothing," Mercedes said as she exited his truck.

"Mercedes, I've been waiting for you. I need to talk to you about Vacation Bible School." Gladys tapped her foot. Mercedes sighed. The woman was worked up about something.

"I wanted to talk to you as well, Gladys," Mercedes said softly. "Let's talk over here, away from the door." They moved to the left side of the porch.

Gladys crossed her arms and opened her mouth to speak, but Mercedes interrupted her.

"Before you say anything, I just wanted you to know that I didn't mean to railroad your Vacation Bible School meeting. I should have talked to you first to get your perspective on the new ideas. You have been doing this ministry for years, and I value your opinion."

Gladys unfolded her arms. "Thank you, Mercedes. I appreciate that. I truly do. I've been thinking a lot since Chase passed away. Some of us oldies have been doing these ministries for years, and we may not be here much longer. You are right about the youth. They must come alongside us and learn how to do things."

Mercedes smiled. "I'm so glad to hear you say that. You never know, Gladys; they might even teach you a thing or two."

Gladys sniffed. "We'll see about that." She then smiled and linked her elbow through Mercedes's arm. "Come inside with me. I've got some new floral arrangement ideas for the sanctuary."

"I can't wait to hear them." Mercedes smiled back and then did a double take as they walked in. Mark Wildmen sat in the first row of the auditorium. "Excuse me, Gladys. Let me greet this visitor. I'll get with you about the floral arrangements later."

She crossed over and shook his hand. "Mark, it's good to see you here tonight. How are you after yesterday's ordeal?"

"I'm doing well. Yesterday was pretty crazy. That man just disappearing like that got me thinking—what if he was an angel? Maybe I need to take another look at this God thing. I found my dad's Bible at home last night. There are some verses underlined by him. Not very many. He wasn't very religious, but it's still pretty cool—almost like he's showing me something from beyond the grave." Mark wiped at the tears beginning to pool.

"That's awesome, Mark. I'll be praying for you to find what you are looking for." Mercedes put her hand on his shoulder.

"Thanks. At first, I wanted to be a better man for Alice, but I realized I needed to be better for myself."

Mercedes felt her heart melt a little. He could be so perfect for Alice. *Lord, please show him Your way. Help him to trust in You.*

"Mark, welcome back. Glad I didn't scare you away last time." Grant reached out and shook Mark's hand.

"Nope. I just told Mercedes I'm having a change of heart on all this God stuff. I even found my dad's Bible."

"That's great. I'm proud of you. If you have any questions about anything, feel free to ask. I'll do my best to help."

"Thanks, I'm bound to have some. I'm not very smart when it comes to reading and book stuff," Mark said, his cheeks coloring slightly as he ruffled his hair.

"I think you'll be surprised how easy some of it is to understand," Grant said.

"Mark, you came back!" Alice smiled as she pushed through Mercedes and Grant.

"Pardon me, let us move out of your way," Mercedes said dryly.

"Sorry, I just wanted to make sure my eyes weren't deceiving me. Mark Wildmen is in church again and sitting in the front row! Mark, your wild reputation is down the tank now."

"That's fine; let them talk." Mark laughed. "Are you going to join me in the front row?"

Alice pursed her lips. "You know how there's a splash zone at the Sea Life Park—certain seats that are guaranteed to get wet?"

"I know where you're going with this." Grant pointed his finger at her. "I don't spit when I preach, Alice."

"You've never been on the receiving end! I'm telling you, Mark, you sit there, and you'll get a steam facial."

"Okay, you've convinced me. I'll move to the second row."

"Thanks a lot, Alice." Grant crossed his arms.

"I think it's time for the service to start," Mercedes urged Grant to the platform.

As she listened to her husband's preaching on grace, Mercedes realized she had never given the topic much thought. The parishioners of Shady Lake had given her a lot of grace as a new pastor's wife and someone not that far in her walk with the Lord. *Do I give enough grace to those who have wronged me? I must admit, I'm much more apt to keep grudges.* She focused again on her husband's words and recognized the verses from Romans.

"Even the righteousness of God which is by faith of Jesus Christ unto all and upon all them that believe: for there is no difference: for all have sinned, and come short of the glory of God; Being justified freely by his grace through the redemption that is in Christ Jesus:" Grant paused. "Did you hear that? There is no difference, it's an even playing field—we are all sinners. If you think you are the best, God doesn't care. If you think you are the worst, He doesn't care. He sent His son Jesus to die for us all, so we can have His righteousness, His holiness. We have access to God, to a joy-filled life, and everlasting life in Heaven. Without Christ, we are left with a life of loneliness, despair, and an eternity of pain and torment. Will you accept His precious gift of grace? Will you accept Christ today as your Lord and Savior?"

Grant asked the congregation to stand and invited people to come pray at the altar. Mercedes held her breath, thinking Mark might come forward, but he wasn't among the ones who knelt in prayer.

Later that evening, she spoke to her husband about it as she warmed one of Bertie's scones in the toaster oven.

"What did you think about Mark tonight? I thought for sure he would come forward during the invitation." Mercedes slathered some butter on her scone.

"I did too. I don't know. Maybe he wasn't sure what to do or was embarrassed. Just keep praying for him. You can tell the Lord is working on him. Are you enjoying that scone?" Grant smiled.

Mercedes closed her eyes at the sweet, buttery bite. "It's delicious," she said with a mouth full of crumbs.

CHAPTER 12

Mark

"Dad, what are you doing here? Am I dead?" Mark's father smiled at him and reached out his hand. Mark took a step forward and paused. There were so many things he wanted to tell his dad. He ran to embrace him when something sharp grabbed hold of his leg. His knees buckled from the searing pain, and he stared down in shock as gruesome claws tore into him. The ground where he knelt opened wide, and he began to fall into darkness. He reached around, trying to grasp anything to keep him from descending farther into the earth.

"Mark!" He looked up, his dad's eyes stared down at him in horror. They were the last thing he saw as heavy blackness overtook him.

Mark sat up in bed, gasping for breath. The alarm clock read four in the morning. There was no way he could sleep after that nightmare. He watched the minute hand click by while he sat there, unable to move. *If you had gone to talk to Grant last night, maybe you'd be getting better sleep.* At five, he forced himself out of bed and started some coffee.

"Morning, Mom," he said as his mother walked into the kitchen in her robe and gown.

"G'morning, hon. You are up early." She kissed him on the cheek.

"Yeah, I got lots to do at the shop today. A few items sold through our online store and tons more to catalog."

"That's great. The online store is already working. I knew you would be able to turn this around." She hugged him tightly.

"Thanks, Mom. We still have a lot of work to do. I might also stop to talk to Pastor Grant today." He poured some creamer into his coffee.

"Oh, what do you need to talk to him about? I didn't think you liked church. Does this have anything to do with his sister Alice?" She winked at him.

"No, Mom, it's more spiritual guidance," he said.

"Oh, is that why you wanted your daddy's Bible?" His mother walked a few steps into the adjoining living room and settled in her brown recliner.

"Yeah, I didn't even know he cared about things like that. I don't recall him reading his Bible or praying." He handed his mom a cup of coffee and sat in what used to be his dad's recliner.

Not much had changed in the house he grew up in. Brown wood paneling from the 1980s lined the wall. A prized razorback head hung centered between two mounted deer heads. His dad had updated the floor, replacing the brown linoleum with ceramic tile.

"If he read his Bible, it would be at night while y'all slept. Sometimes, we would read it together. It wasn't often though. One of my regrets as a parent is that we didn't put much emphasis on God. I should have taken you and your brother to church more regularly. Your dad usually was working or hunting. Wrangling you and your brother during a church service seemed like much more work than it was worth." She grabbed a tissue and dabbed her eyes at the memory. "I can see now that it would have been worth it. Maybe it wouldn't have been as hard for you to find yourself or your purpose. I feel like I failed you in so many ways. I'm so proud of the man you have become."

Mark felt a lump gather in his throat. He couldn't remember the last time his mom had ever said she was proud of him. He had always told himself he didn't care, but as he sat with his mom, he knew he never wanted to disappoint her again like he had in the past.

"Mom, have you accepted Christ as your Savior? And did Dad?" Mark asked softly. He wished with all his heart they had—especially his dad because it was too late for him now if he hadn't.

"I did when I was a girl at church. I don't know why I didn't do that with you boys. I'm so mad at myself for not including God in our family."

"You did the best you could, Mom. I think we are in a good place." *At least my brother is.* "What about Dad?" He swallowed hard, nervous about her answer.

His mom smiled. "Your dad trusted Christ as a teenager. I do know that. We just lost our way through the years."

"You are welcome to come with me to church on Sunday," Mark said.

"I'd like that." His mom reached out and squeezed his hand.

After he finished his coffee with his mother, Mark messaged Grant to ask if he had time to talk to him that day.

Grant immediately responded and told him to stop by the church before work. *I could save time by calling and talking to him on the phone.* He hated talking on the phone. Mark sighed as he pulled on his jeans and his lucky T-shirt. He was ready to get this settled once and for all.

He got into his truck and started down the long driveway like he had done a thousand times before. As he rounded a curve to merge onto a dirt road, he grabbed for his seat belt buckle. Before he could fasten it around him, a buck dashed out in front of the truck. Mark jerked the wheel hard left, causing the front end of his truck to nosedive into a deep ditch. A blast of pain erupted from the impact of the airbags releasing. He heard the seat belt slap back into place. *Too late*, he thought before he passed out.

Grant couldn't have been happier than when he received Mark's text. He just knew Mark was ready to take that next step in faith. He texted Mercedes to tell her he was meeting with Mark and to pray, then hurried over to the church. Whistling the tune to "At Calvary," he started a fresh pot of coffee.

"Someone's happy today," a voice came from behind him.

"Harold, how are you, friend?" Grant turned and hugged him. He immediately felt guilty for his happiness in the shadow of the passing of their dearest friend. "Mark Wildmen is on his way to talk to me. I think he is finally ready to trust Christ."

"Then that is a cause for some joy," Harold said, smiling sadly. "Chase would want us to be happy."

"How are you holding up?" Grant poured a cup of coffee and passed it to his friend.

"I would like to say I'm fine, but I'm not. I miss my friend. We talked to each other every day, you know. He was more like a brother to me than my own brother." Harold wiped his eyes with his handkerchief. "I didn't cry at all yesterday, but today it's like I can't stop."

"It's okay not to be okay. It's okay not to be fine. Cry, yell if you need to. I think this may be the hardest funeral I have to conduct," Grant said.

"No, the hardest funeral to preach is to the families who've lost a loved one who never trusted Christ. We at least have hope in knowing we will see Chase again. Those people hold nothing but memories," Harold sipped his coffee.

"What are your plans today?" Grant asked, ready to move on from the funeral talk.

"I'm meeting Daniel, the Rossi's boy, and one of his friends. They are going to help me with the mowing and weed eating. Give them something else to do during the summer. Gladys and the ladies are coming to clean and straighten the sanctuary for the funeral."

"That's great. I'm going to take my coffee to my office and wait for Mark to arrive. He should be here any minute. If you need help with the boys after we finish talking, let me know," Grant offered.

"I might take you up on that. I'm not sure how much work these boys have done before." Harold smiled, and Grant recognized the glint of light he had come so much to love in his friend.

"Sure thing," he said.

Grant returned to his office and started working on his sermon for Sunday. After some time passed, he stretched and glanced at his clock. An hour had gone by. There were no messages on his phone. Puzzled, he tried Mark's number. No answer. He tried the shop number. No answer. He looked up Wildmen in the white pages online and found what he hoped was his mother's number. There weren't very many Wildmens in Shady Springs. He dialed the number, and a woman answered on the other end.

"Hello?"

"Hi, is this Lorna Wildmen, Mark Wildmen's mother?"

"Yes, it is. Can I help you?" The woman sounded confused.

"This is Pastor Grant Ford. Mark was supposed to meet with me this morning but never showed. I've tried his cell and the shop number. Do you know where he is?"

"Pastor Grant, I know he left this house to see you. If he didn't make it there, then something terrible has happened. I can't get out and drive because of my knees. Can you drive the route from the church to our house? We live out in the boondocks. If he's in trouble, no one's going to find him. Please, Pastor."

Grant rubbed his temple. This was not how he had planned his day. He grabbed his keys and started towards the door. "Yes, ma'am. I'll head out that way now."

Fastening his helmet, he revved up his Harley and said a silent prayer. *Lord, please let Mark be all right, and if he's in trouble, let me get there in time.*

Mark lived only ten minutes away. Since there was only one way to get to Mark's house, Grant felt confident in the route he took. He turned off the paved street to a dirt road and slowed down. A pit formed in his stomach as Grant approached the long driveway to Mark's house. The front end of Mark's truck had nosedived into the deep ditch running along the road. The pine trees along the road obscured the view to anyone in the house.

He skidded to a stop by the truck, grabbed his phone, and dialed 9-1-1. He ran to the driver's side, praying he was alive.

"Mark, are you okay? Mark?"

Mark sat unresponsive. Blood flowed from his temple and signs of bruising were appearing on his face. Grant pushed the airbag back and felt for a pulse. Relief rushed over him.

"He's alive." He replied to the dispatcher's onslaught of questions. "There's a pulse, but it's faint. The ambulance needs to hurry. Please hurry." He rattled off the Wildmens' address and laid the phone on the dashboard with the speaker still on.

"Mark, Mark? Can you hear me?" Grant didn't want to touch his head or neck in case of injuries, but he wanted Mark to be conscious. Mark groaned.

"Where am I?" Mark opened an eye and quickly shut it in pain. He sat completely still.

"Right outside your driveway, somehow you and your truck ended up in a ditch," Grant explained.

"Deer," Mark said.

"There was a deer?" Grant said.

"Yes. Is the other dude here? Hurts to talk," Mark said. A tear trickled down his cheek.

"I'm the only person here. You don't have to talk, bud. Just stay awake, okay? You need to stay awake," Grant repeated.

"Jesus. Need Jesus, Grant." Mark opened his eyes, panicked.

"Jesus is here for you, Mark. All you have to do is believe and trust Him as your Savior. Do you believe?"

"Yes, I believe in Jesus. I trust Him as my Savior," Mark gasped. "Tell Alice. I'm sorry."

"Oh no, you don't. You old dog. You are going to tell her that yourself. You stay awake, and you tell her that yourself."

Mark smiled and grimaced. Grant wiped his eyes. *Please, Lord. Don't let him die.*

A siren wailed close, and Grant silently thanked the Lord. He couldn't believe the ambulance had made it there so fast.

"Mark, the ambulance is here. It's here. Just hold on a little bit longer." He stepped away from the vehicle to let the paramedics do their thing.

"The ambulance is here," he told the dispatcher. "How did it get here so fast?"

"Before you called, we had an anonymous caller say there had been a wreck, and it looked like the person might be hurt. The caller didn't stay on the line but gave us the address before he disconnected."

"Mark asked if there was someone else here. Maybe he'll remember who it was later," Grant said thoughtfully. He ended the call with dispatch and went to get Mark's mother.

After he explained the situation, he helped her get in her car and drove her down the driveway just as the paramedics closed the ambulance's back doors.

"Are y'all taking him to Shady Springs Hospital?" Grant asked one of the paramedics from the driver's side window. If the situation were severe, sometimes they transferred residents to a larger hospital in Cedar Ridge.

"For now. We will have to see what the X-rays show. They might transfer him later. He's pretty out of it. There may be some internal damage." The man got into the ambulance, and they followed behind.

"Was he conscious at all? Were you able to speak to him?" Tears were streaming down Lorna's face.

"A little bit. Mark said he was in a lot of pain, and it hurt to talk. When I left him with the paramedics, he was still conscious." Grant tried to reassure her.

"Did he get to talk to you about faith at all?" she whispered as she stared vacantly out the window.

"Yes, he did, and he professed Christ as his Savior." Grant watched her shoulders sag in relief as she whispered a thank you.

"First my husband's death and now my son's accident. This hasn't been my best year. I don't know how much more I can handle. It's too much."

"The Lord will give you what you need to get through this. We'll help you. Sammy? That's your other son, right? I know he will help too," Grant said.

"Why would you help me? I'm not even a part of your congregation. I haven't done anything to deserve your generosity." Lorna sniffed.

Grant pulled into the hospital behind the ambulance. "That's just what grace is. We don't do anything to earn it.

It's just given to us. God gives us more grace so we can give to others."

He let her out at the emergency doors so she could walk in with her son while he parked her car. He called Mercedes as he walked back to the hospital and filled her in on the situation.

"I'm glad you could talk to him before the paramedics arrived. It's wild. We just saw him last night at church. Did you call Alice?"

"No, do you think I should?" Grant hadn't even thought of calling his sister.

"Um, yes. Whether Alice wants to admit it or not, something is going on there," Mercedes said.

"Can you call her? I've got to check in with his mom." *I really don't want to talk to my sister about a possible boyfriend.* Mercedes agreed to call Alice, and Grant went to find Mrs. Wildmen to get the latest update on Mark.

She was on the phone with her son, Sammy, when he found her.

"They haven't told us anything yet. They rushed him back for X-rays and tests. We will probably be up here for a while. Pastor Grant drove me here. But if you don't mind stopping by the house and picking up my crochet bag, that will keep my mind busy while we await answers. See you soon."

"Is Sammy headed this way?" Grant asked as they sat down in the almost empty waiting room.

An older gentleman wearing a neck brace sat in the back of the room. Grant gave him a nod, which the man returned with a single wave.

"Yes, he's leaving now. He should be here in about an hour and a half." She sniffed. "Did you call Alice?"

"My wife is calling her."

"I always liked Alice for Mark. She seemed to be the only person who could see who he was." Lorna blew her nose.

Grant didn't know how to respond. He liked Mark, but he was protective of his sister. He didn't want to see her hurt again.

"If you'll excuse me, I need to call some people at church and let them know where I am. Do you mind if I add Mark to our church prayer chain?" He didn't think Lorna would mind, but some people disliked sharing personal information. That was another lesson he learned the hard way.

"That would be wonderful if your church could pray for him. Thank you. I've got a few more people to call myself."

Grant called Harold and told him what had transpired. "Looks like I might be here awhile. Can you get the prayer chain started for Mark?"

As Grant disconnected the call, he made his way to Lorna, confident Harold would take care of the prayer chain and preparations for Chase's funeral. Before he could sit down, a doctor approached them. His heart sank as he took in the woman's somber expression.

CHAPTER 13

Alice

Wouldn't you know?
Aren't you some sort of angel?
—Alice

Alice pressed play on her playlist, determined to clear the other side of the attic. The police escorted Martin Pitrones out of town last night, so she had nothing to fear. Two more boxes of old files and a broken wicker basket went into the trash pile. Some old empty hat boxes and a box of old records went into the donate pile. After finding a few more boxes for the donate pile, she realized another trip to Priceless Junk was in order. She also recognized the flutter of excitement at the mere thought of seeing Mark again. It was getting harder to downplay her feelings for him. She wished she knew where he stood with the Lord. Having the same belief as her partner played a big role in the foundation of their relationship. She blew her hair out of her face as she sent him a text.

Have more stuff. When can I come by?

She tapped her foot impatiently. No response. *Maybe he's with a customer. Don't be one of those girls who always expect an immediate reply.* Making sure her notifications were on, and the volume was high, she got back to work. She pulled a few of the last boxes from the very back. A thick layer of dust covered them. *Gross.* Just the sight of them made her sneeze.

Her phone began to ring.

"Saved by the bell," she muttered. She thought, or rather hoped, it would be Mark calling. Instead, the name Mercedes scrolled across the phone screen.

"What's up Mercedes?" She sat down on the floor away from the dusty boxes, taking a break.

"I've got some bad news, Alice. It's about Mark."

Alice sat upright, frightened by the tone of her voice. "What happened?" she whispered.

"There was an accident. Mark swerved to avoid hitting a deer and ran his truck into a ditch. He's at Shady Springs Hospital. Grant found him and is with him."

"Wait, how did Grant find him? Why didn't he call me?" Alice questioned.

"Mark planned on meeting Grant this morning. He wanted to talk to him about trusting Christ. When Mark didn't show up, Grant got worried and called Lorna, his—"

"His mom, yes, I know," Alice said impatiently.

"Of course, sorry. Anyway, Lorna asked your brother to drive over to look for him since she hadn't been able to get out of the house," Mercedes said calmly.

For some reason, the calmness irritated her further. "But why didn't Grant call me?" she demanded.

"I don't think he realized how you felt about Mark. I mean, you've been denying any sort of relationship with him, Alice."

She closed her eyes and breathed deeply. Mercedes was right, of course. She was acting like a crazy person.

"I'm sorry. I'm just upset and taking it out on you. Do you think it's okay if I go up there?"

"Absolutely," Mercedes encouraged.

"Okay, I'm going to head down to the hospital. If you hear any updates, will you call me?" Alice stood and wiped the dust bunnies off her jeans.

"Sure will," Mercedes promised.

As she drove to the hospital, tears began to fall. "Why God? He was so close to trusting you. Why did you let this happen? It's not fair." When she pulled into the parking lot, she reined in her emotions and walked calmly to the glass doors. *You can do this, girl. Breathe.* The doors to the emergency room opened. A doctor stood talking to Grant and Lorna. Lorna sobbed, and Grant wrapped his arms around her. Alice froze in her tracks. She turned and ran out before anyone could notice her.

"It's too much. I can't handle this." She ran across the parking lot to some benches overlooking the lake and sobbed out loud.

The sun shone hot and bright, blinding her eyes as she knelt on the grass beside the bench. *Why didn't I tell him how I felt? Why didn't I push him more to trust Christ earlier? Is he in hell now because of me?* Her stomach lurched at the thought. She wiped her eyes and hugged her body.

"Are you all right, Alice?"

Startled, she jumped to her feet and whirled around. The man from the cabin sat on the bench. "What are you doing here?"

"I had a snake bite, remember? That sun sure is bright today." The man grinned, squinting up at her.

"B-But you disappeared from the cabin. Th-They looked everywhere for you," she stammered. *Am I losing my mind? Is this real?* she thought to herself as she rubbed her eyes.

"Sometimes, what you are looking for is staring you right in the face, but that's not why you are out here crying, is it?" he said gently.

"No, my friend Mark crashed his car. You know him. He let you borrow his camera. Anyway, he didn't make it." She sniffed.

"Oh yes, I remember Mark. Very compassionate man. Are you sure he didn't make it?"

"Wouldn't you know? Aren't you some sort of angel?" She didn't care if he called her crazy. Her life was turned upside down, and it was time for some answers.

"Bold. I like it. I would say don't be afraid—it's our catch-phrase—but I don't think you feel scared right now." He gave her a wink.

"I'm not afraid. I want answers, and I want Mark to be okay. Am I cursed? Did this happen because of me?" She looked at her feet, terrified of his response.

"You are blessed, Alice." She looked up at him in shock as her phone started to ring. She signaled to him this wasn't over and turned to answer, not checking to see who was calling.

"Alice? Where are you? Grant called me with news on Mark, and I thought you would already be at the hospital."

"I'm at the hospital. I walked in and saw the doctor telling Grant and Lorna that Mark had died, and I ran out. I couldn't deal with it. And then... The angel, or whatever, is here. He—" She turned to point at the bench and dropped her hand to her side. "He's gone."

"Alice, stop. Listen to me. Mark isn't gone. Okay? He isn't dead. The doctor said he was in a coma, and he expected him to come out of it in the next few days."

Alice tried to process Mercedes' words. *Mark was alive. He was in a coma.* The thoughts of her park bench visitor flew out of her mind.

"Mercedes, what if he doesn't wake up? He never accepted Christ as his Savior. If he dies and goes to hell, that is on me. I should have urged him more." Alice wiped a tear from her cheek.

"But he did trust Christ, Alice," Mercedes said.

"What do you mean? He crashed before he could talk to Grant," Alice argued.

"When Grant found him, he was conscious and accepted Christ as his Savior," Mercedes explained.

She wiped away some more hot tears and sniffled.

"Go inside the hospital, Alice. Go to your brother," Mercedes urged.

"Okay. Thank you, Mercedes."

"Love you, Alice." She could hear the warmth in her sister-in-law's voice.

"Love you too."

She ran across the parking lot and through the hospital's emergency entrance. Grant and Lorna sat beside each other.

"Hey," she said.

Grant looked at her in concern, and she saw why as she took in her reflection in the hospital window. Her face, red and sweaty from crying and being out in the heat, along with her dirty clothes from working in the attic, gave her the appearance of a literal hot mess.

He crossed over to her and hugged her dirty, sweaty self.

"I was worried about you. Mercedes said you should have been here a while ago. What happened? Are you okay?" He held her at arm's length and studied her.

"I'm fine. I arrived earlier, but when I came in, I saw you hugging Lorna while the doctor was talking to you. She cried so much, I thought Mark had passed. I couldn't breathe, so I walked to the lake to get some air and think. I had no idea what was going on until Mercedes called me."

"I'm so sorry you thought he died. That's horrible. Come sit down. I'm waiting with Lorna until her son, Sammy, gets here." Grant motioned toward the chairs.

"I will. Let me clean up first. I didn't realize what a mess I was till I saw your reaction and my reflection." She grimaced.

"Okay, we will be waiting over there whenever you're ready," Grant said.

Alice walked to the bathroom and washed her face in the sink. She pulled a brush out of her purse and ran it through her hair a few times before she pulled it back in a ponytail. It was too hot to have her hair on her neck. After patting the remaining dust off her jeans, she washed her hands and arms. Feeling better about her demeanor, she returned to the waiting room to sit with Grant and Lorna.

"Thank you for coming up here, Alice. Mark thinks highly of you, and I know he'd be pleased you are here. When Sammy arrives, we will work up a rotation to sit with Mark until he wakes up. I'd like one of us to be here, so he doesn't wake up alone. Would you want to be a part of the rotation?" Lorna asked.

"Yes, I'd love to help any way I can. Thanks for including me," Alice said.

"Thank you." Lorna squeezed her knee. "I know you both remember Mark as a wild teen, and it's true—Mark could sniff out trouble like a hound dog. As a child though, he was very thoughtful and hated disappointing me or his father. One time, he broke a vase and cried and cried. I didn't even have to scold him. He'd punish himself. He didn't start acting out until later in school—never hurt anyone, though. I can tell he's trying to turn his life around now. He's stubborn enough to see it through too." Lorna smiled.

"He's stubborn, all right," a voice spoke behind them.

"Sammy, you made it." Lorna rose and hugged her younger son. He handed her a bag of yarn and large crochet hooks. "Thanks for bringing me my bag. Do you remember Alice?"

"Of course, it's good to see you again, Alice."

Alice nodded, feeling shy. *Had Mark told Sammy anything about her?*

"Hi, I'm Alice's brother, Grant Ford." Grant shook Sammy's hand.

"Grant, as in Pastor Grant? Mark spoke to me about you. Thanks for helping him. He can be a knucklehead sometimes," Sammy said.

"I think you'd be proud of him. I talked to him before the paramedics arrived, and he was coherent enough to profess Christ as his Savior," Grant said, smiling.

"I'm so relieved to hear that. I made that decision a few years ago and have been praying for Mark ever since. That is awesome," Sammy said.

"We've just been sitting around waiting. Your mom has been telling us what Mark was like as a boy." Alice motioned to the chairs.

"He was a great big brother. Sure, we got in trouble, but it was harmless. He always had my back. I wish he had stayed in touch," Sammy said.

"He stood up for me at school—even fought the school bully." Alice smiled at the memory.

"You never told me about that," Grant said.

"That's because you're my brother, and I don't tell you everything." Alice rolled her eyes.

"Excuse me," the doctor interrupted.

"Has he woken up?" Lorna asked. She grabbed Alice's hand tightly.

"No, ma'am, but we have gotten him into a room now, and you all can go see him one at a time. Remember he has some bruised ribs, so don't go hugging him. He is in room 211," she explained.

"Thank you, Doctor," Lorna said.

The doctor nodded and walked over to speak to an orderly.

"Let's all take a turn seeing him, and then I'll stay till visiting hours are over," Lorna instructed.

"Do you want me to pick you up then? How are you going to get home?" Sammy said, smiling.

"Of course, you are going to pick me up. And then you can stay tomorrow," Lorna said.

"Mom, I have a test tomorrow. If Alice can come on Friday, I'll come up Friday night and stay on Saturday and Sunday. Would that work?"

Lorna shook her head and grasped Sammy's hand. "I forgot about your classes. I'm sorry, Sammy. Would you be able to sit with Mark tomorrow, Alice?"

"Sure. My summer schedule is super flexible," Alice assured her.

"Good. Let's pray he wakes up by this weekend, and if not, we will figure the rest out then."

Alice waited outside the door as Lorna and then Sammy entered the room where Mark lay. They both left the room visibly shaken. Sammy shook his head with tears in his eyes.

"I've never seen my brother so still."

She held her breath, scared of the version of Mark that awaited her in the hospital room. *Will I even be able to recognize him?* She breathed a sigh of relief at the bandage wrapped around his temple and badly bruised face. *He still looks like my Mark,* she thought to herself. She reached over and took his hand.

"Hey, Mark, I hope you can hear me. We are all here rooting for you. Quit mucking around and come out of this. It's rude to keep us waiting." Scanning his face for any response and finding none, she leaned in and whispered in his ear, "Mark, I've got some things I want to say to you I know you would want to hear, but you must wake up. I'm waiting for you." She gently squeezed his hand and walked to where the others were waiting.

CHAPTER 14

Alice

*Since I learned about Christ and His love for me, I know that I
do have worth.*
—Mark

The next morning, Alice threw a couple of books and snacks into her bag and headed out the door for her turn at the hospital. This evening would be Chase's viewing. Sitting at the hospital alone in her thoughts did not sound like fun. Hopefully, her favorite author could help keep her mind off things.

When she reached room 211, she took in the empty, disheveled bed. *Of course, even in a coma, Mark wouldn't be where he's supposed to be.*

"Excuse me," she called out to a passing nurse, "Do you know where the man from this room is?"

The nurse grabbed the clipboard on the wall and scanned it.

"It doesn't say. I don't know."

"He had broken ribs, so I know he didn't just walk out of here." Alice tried to keep the annoyance out of her voice.

"Sorry," the nurse shrugged and continued on her way.

Alice took a deep breath and headed to the nurses station. Surely one of them would know what was going on. A man and two women sat behind the counter.

"Excuse me, I came to visit with Mark Wildmen in room 211, but he's not there. Do you know where he is? He is in a coma."

"Mark? He's a funny fellow. Had me howling last night." The man slapped his knee, laughing.

"Kurt?" Alice squinted at the nurse's badge, failing to see the humor in the situation. She tried to remain calm and spoke slowly. "Are you saying Mark is awake? Nobody's called the family."

"I'm sorry, I'm not sure why no one was notified. He woke up around three in the morning, and I sat with him for a while. Boy, he can sure tell some stories."

"Sounds like Mark." Alice felt relief wash over her at the thought of him awake and in good humor.

"I think he wanted to get a wheelchair so he could be more mobile. If he got a wheelchair, he might have sweet-talked a nurse into pushing him around. Doesn't seem to like sitting still."

"Yeah, he's been that way since grade school. Should I wait in his room then?"

Kurt checked the computer screen. "Sure, I'm not sure how much longer he will last before exhaustion sets in. He must be gettin' tired, and it's almost time for his pain reliever."

Alice pulled her phone out to call Lorna about Mark waking up but stopped. What if the nurse had it wrong? She wanted to see Mark up and talking for herself before she spread the word he was out of the woods. She sat in the chair of his hospital room and stared at the open door, willing him to come through. Giving up hope, she pulled out her book and tried to concentrate on the story.

"Can't this thing go any faster? Just wait till I'm one-hundred-percent, then I'll show you a thing or two." She heard a familiar booming voice come down the hallway.

"You're so bad, Mark," a female voice giggled. Alice rolled her eyes and jammed her book back into her bag.

A blond nurse backed into the room, pulling the wheelchair into it. She wheeled Mark around, and they both stared, mouths agape, at the sight of Alice in the chair.

"Alice, you're here! I'm so glad to see you. There's so much I need to tell you." Mark smiled.

"Your mother put together a rotation schedule for people to sit with you until you woke up. They didn't call anyone to let them know you were awake." Her words came out stiff.

"That's on me," the nurse spoke up. "I was supposed to call all of you, but then Mark got me sidetracked by his great wheelchair escape. You know how he is." She winked at Alice.

Oh, no. This girl did not just wink at me. She could feel the blood rushing to her head.

"Well, I'll go call his mother, so she won't spend the morning worrying." Alice couldn't keep the edge out of her voice as she walked into the hallway.

"I think I'm in trouble," she overheard the nurse say, laughing.

"I didn't know that no one called my family. I know they must have been worrying," Mark replied faintly.

She quickly phoned Lorna and updated her on her son's situation. Then, she stopped and took a deep breath before reentering the room. *Get it together, Alice. Jealousy is never a good look.* As she entered, it took all her strength not to walk back out.

Blondie bent over Mark, plumping his pillows, giving him plenty to look at. Mark shook his head at Alice, eyes wide.

"I think that's it for now." Blondie pulled a slip of paper from the front of her shirt and handed it to Mark. "This is my cell number. It's reserved for very special patients. You can call me anytime."

Alice couldn't believe what she was seeing and hearing. Sure, Mark was a handsome guy, but this was ridiculous. She began to say something, but Mark beat her to it.

"I'm sorry, but I can't accept that. My heart belongs to someone else. I'm sorry if I led you to believe there was something more."

"Whatever. It's your loss." The nurse shrugged and fled the room without making eye contact.

"You sure do make friends fast." Alice forced a smile. *If he had taken that number, he would have had more injuries.*

His face turned red. "I hate sitting in hospitals. I feel like I'm trapped."

"I get that. Your mom said she'll be around later today. A friend is going to give her a ride. You gave us all a scare, Mark." She stood by his bed and shifted her feet.

"Come sit over here, there's plenty of room." Mark patted the bed by his side.

She hesitated and sat on the very edge, careful not to move the bed.

"Ow," he grabbed his chest, and she jumped.

"I'm so sorry! Are you okay?"

He laughed. "Just kidding, have a seat. I'm sorry. I couldn't help it."

She sat back down in a huff and crossed her arms in front of her. "I should have known."

"I meant it when I said I have things I need to tell you." He took her hand in his.

"I'm listening." She tried to ignore the tingling feeling of his fingers wrapping around hers.

"Alice, I've always thought you were out of my league. That I could never be worthy of someone like you. I thought it was impossible, so I didn't even try. Since I learned about Christ and His love for me, I know that I do have worth. I have a heck of a lot to learn and grow, but I want to do that with you. I love you, Alice. That might scare the heck out of you, but I was never one to hide my feelings. I just lay it all out there. I'll tell that nurse. I'll tell your brother. You have always been the girl for me. I've known it for years, and I will wait for however long it takes for you to feel the same. You don't even need to tell me how you feel right now. I want you to know where I stand. We aren't promised a tomorrow, and we need to share what is in our hearts today. That's one lesson I've learned from all this."

Alice sat speechless. The two stared at each other. His words and heart were so sincere. He had shared his heart and soul, and although he didn't ask her to share hers, she knew she had to reciprocate.

"I've never thought you unworthy or less of a man, Mark. If anything, I've always admired how you think differently from others. You have a wonderful heart and make me laugh. I love how you've stepped up to help your family and decided to trust Christ. When I'm with you, it's like I'm with an old friend. When you left me, I didn't think I mattered to you. I was just another girl who fell for Mark Wildmen. And I can't deny it, even though I try, I am still falling for you."

His whole face lit up. "You've no idea how happy I am right now. My truck is totaled, my body is in pain, but right now I am the happiest guy alive."

"Hope I'm not breaking up something here." Grant popped his head into the hospital room.

"There is no breaking up allowed here." Mark placed his other hand on top of hers.

"Hmm. Okay." Grant side-eyed their hands as he entered the room. "It's good to see you up and talking, Mark."

"Thank you so much for coming to find me. You saved my life."

"Do you remember anything from yesterday morning? The dispatcher said she received an anonymous call before I got to you. That's how they got there so quickly. You asked me about another guy when I found you." Grant sat down in the chair on the other side of the bed.

"I remember driving and then the deer. There was a horrible crashing sound and darkness. Then someone called my name, and there was a light. I saw these bright eyes, and someone touched my forehead. Then I blacked out again. The next thing I remember is you asking me if I would believe and accept Jesus, which I did." He smiled and squeezed Alice's hand. "Who or what do you think that was? Do you think it was an angel, Grant?"

"The Bible says we might be entertaining angels unaware. There are also a couple of instances in the Old Testament where two men enter towns, and they are, in reality, angels. Humans would mistake the angels for men. So, yes. I think there is a real possibility you were with an angel." Grant leaned back in the chair.

"I think these testers have been angels. Yesterday, when I was out by the lake, the same guy who was in Judd Hart's Cabin appeared behind me on a bench. I was so frustrated with everything going on that I asked him if he was an angel. He told me he would normally tell me not to be afraid; that was their catchphrase." Alice shifted so she could see Grant's reaction.

"That's what angels say a lot to the people they appeared to in the Bible!" Grant stood with excitement. "Wait, why didn't you mention this yesterday?"

"I was kind of focused on one thing." Alice felt her face grow hot.

"Must have been something important," Mark teased.

"Actually, yes, someone significant." Alice smiled at him.

"Oh brother, is this how it will be from now on?" Grant complained.

Alice wagged her finger at him. "Oh no, don't you even start! I've endured you and Mercedes mooning all over each other for months."

"Whatever." Grant ignored her and began to pace the room. "Think about what we've experienced. Every one of us has encountered an angel over the past week. Do you know how incredible that is? Did the angel say anything else yesterday, Alice?" Grant stopped pacing and refocused on his sister.

"I asked him if I was cursed, and he said I was blessed. Then Mercedes called me on the phone. When I turned back to talk to him, he had disappeared. Isn't their MO disappearing into thin air? Angel MO? Is there such a thing?" Alice asked.

"I think *modus operandi* refers to criminal behavior. Maybe not the best way to describe an angel if you want to stay on their good side," Mark said.

Grant tapped the metal bars of Mark's bedframe. "Regardless, we've all experienced something pretty miraculous. I'm glad you're doing well, Mark. I still have some things to do to take care of Chase's viewing and the funeral tomorrow, so I'd better get going."

"I wish I had gotten a chance to know him better. We had a brief encounter at church on Sunday. He seemed like a pretty stand-up guy," Mark said.

"He was an amazing man who loved the Lord and loved people. I don't know what I'm going to do without him." Grant gave them a sad smile as he left.

At the mention of Chase's name, Alice felt tears begin to well.

"Are you all right?" Mark looked at her with concern.

"It's Chase. It will take some time for me to realize he is gone. He's been a part of my family's life for so long. I feel like I've lost my father all over again." Alice grabbed a tissue from the side table.

"Losing a dad is hard. It's something I know all about. At least you had a good relationship before he passed, you know. That's something I can never get back with my dad." Mark grimaced and held his side. "I think my pain medicine has done wore off. Can you hit that button for the nurse?" He pointed to a button on the side of the bed.

"It better not be Blondie again," Alice warned as she pressed the button.

"Blondie?" Mark laughed and then winced again. "Ow, don't make me laugh."

"I bet you want to take some of these right about now." Kurt popped his head in the doorframe and shook a bottle of pills.

"Yes, please," Mark said. Beads of sweat began to cluster on his brow. Alice jumped out of the nurse's way.

"You've overdone it, Mark. You are going to have to slow down. No more wheelchair escapes," she admonished.

"I agree with your girl, Mark—time to rest. You've got to heal," Kurt handed him his meds with his water and checked his stats.

When Kurt finished and left, Mark motioned for Alice to sit beside him again.

"You heard the nurse, you need to rest," she said.

"Please just sit and hold my hand until I fall asleep," Mark begged.

Alice laughed and obliged. He was out in five minutes. She sat and watched him sleep for a moment before she returned to her chair in the corner.

Her phone lit up with a text from Mercedes, and she smiled as she read it.

Grant told me you were at the hospital and Mark is awake! He also said you two looked cozy. I want all the details later!

She replied with a smiling wink emoji and pulled out her book to read. When Mark's mother arrived, he was still sleeping. Alice told Lorna about his wheelchair antics, minus the flirting nurse, and left her with her son. *Now, if only I can get through Chase's viewing without becoming a blubbering mess,* Alice thought to herself.

CHAPTER 15

Mercedes

Would she be more mindful of people around her and their needs?
—Mercedes

"Alice, Carol, are you ready to go?" Mercedes called from Carol's entryway. Grant had to be at the church early to prepare for the viewing, so she had decided to ride with his family. Alice and Carol came out with yellow rose corsages pinned to their dresses.

"What are the yellow roses for?" Mercedes asked.

"Yellow roses were Chase's favorite flower. We got one for you too," Alice said.

Mercedes touched the soft petals and pinned them to her navy dress. "That's so thoughtful of you. What a lovely idea."

The three women froze for a moment. Time stood still as they realized the finality of this night.

Alice looks terrified. Mercedes realized she must also look terrified as Carol took both women in her arms and spoke reassuringly to them.

"This will be hard. We all loved Chase. But he is in much better shape now. You girls know he was slowing down. He is with his wife and so many of his friends and family who have already passed on. Most of all, he is with his Lord. Chase wants us to be happy. He wouldn't want us to be sad for long."

They piled into Mercedes' car and drove to the funeral home.

"What is even the purpose of a viewing? When I am dead, I don't want someone looking at my dead body." Alice wrinkled her nose.

"It's for the deceased's loved ones to have a sense of closure. I once went to a viewing postponed a week or two so a loved one could fly in. The body had already decomposed a little. It was not the lasting memory I wanted of that person," Carol said.

"Yikes. Let's lighten the mood with an Alice and Mark update!" Mercedes said brightly.

"Mercedes!" Alice glared at her.

"You can glare away, Alice, but we need some answers." Mercedes smiled.

"Fine, so I went to the hospital, and Mark basically declared his love for me. What can I say? The boy is smitten." Alice examined her fingernails.

"Summer loving, having some fun. . ." Mercedes sang. She watched Alice turn bright red. It seemed cruel, but after all

Alice's teasing toward her, this was the perfect time for a bit of payback.

"Mercedes Lewis. I know you didn't just burst out in the *Grease* song." Alice crossed her arms.

"Tell me more, tell me more, tell me more," her mother joined in, and they all laughed.

The laughter felt like a sunbeam bursting through the storm clouds in Mercedes' heart.

"Come on, Alice, what did you say after he professed his undying love? How do you feel about him?" Mercedes asked once they had gotten themselves together.

"I told him I was falling for him," Alice said in a small voice.

"Aw," Mercedes and her mother both sighed simultaneously.

"I'm so happy for you." Mercedes sighed.

"What about you, Mom? Do you think it's too soon?" Alice said.

Carol turned in her seat and smiled at her daughter. "You two have known each other for years. I'm impressed how Mark stepped up and helped his mom. Now that he has decided to accept Christ, I'm excited to see him grow in the Lord. Christ strengthens the bond in any relationship."

As Mercedes pulled into the funeral home, her sunbeam disintegrated inside, and the heavy storm clouds pulled at her heart. She fingered the velvety petals on her rose and breathed back the tears that threatened to stream down her face. "When you're ready to go, just let me know. We don't have to stay the entire time." The three agreed and walked under a large green awning into a white brick building.

Mercedes spotted her husband talking to one of the funeral home directors. "There you are." She hugged him and kissed his cheek.

He squeezed her tightly. "I'm so glad you're here." His red-rimmed eyes began to water. "There's a sign-in sheet over there if you want to sign us in. I've already gone in to see him, but if you want me to go in with you, come and get me."

Mercedes glanced at the other signatures as she signed their names. The viewing started twenty minutes ago, and she estimated about thirty people had signed already. She peered in where the viewing took place. An open casket framed by floral arrays of lilies and roses sat in the center of the room. Burgundy chairs lined the center aisle. People sat or milled about in hushed clusters, talking. Quiet piano music played overhead, and a slideshow of Chase from his toddler days to recent photos played in a loop. A picture flashed of her, Grant, and Chase on their wedding day, and her vision blurred. *He was such a sweet, dear man.*

"Did you enjoy the strawberry scones?" Gertie spoke up beside her.

"Yes, ma'am. They were delicious. Are you doing okay?" Mercedes tried to blink her tears away and hugged the woman.

"Yes, it seems like the older you get, the more of these you attend." Gertie wiped her eye with a kerchief.

"Ready?" Mercedes felt a tug on her elbow and turned to see her husband.

They walked hand in hand down to the casket. Chase wore a black suit, and a yellow rose rested on his breast pocket.

"He looks peaceful," Mercedes pulled out a tissue from her purse and dabbed her eyes. "We are going to miss you, Chase."

"Excuse me," a voice said softly behind them.

"Oh, sorry. We didn't mean to get in your way." She moved to the other side of the casket.

"Actually, I wanted to talk to you. Are you the pastor of Shady Springs church?" The woman gestured toward Grant.

"I am, and this is my wife, Mercedes," Grant said.

"Nice to meet you. My name is Helen Dimpsey. Chase was my uncle." She shook their hands.

Mercedes studied the woman. Helen's auburn hair was pulled back in a sleek updo. She wore a tailored dress suit and designer handbag that would have cost one month of Mercedes' salary.

"Chase spoke highly of you and the church the few times I talked with him on the phone. I just found out he left me his house in Shady Springs. It surprised me. It's been so long since I've visited him. I stayed a few summers with him and my aunt when I was little. They were some of the best summers I ever had. We would spend all day swimming and fishing at the lake. My aunt would make the most delicious desserts." Her eyes softened at the memory.

"For him to leave you his home, he must've known how much you enjoyed your time there," Grant said.

Helen dabbed her eye with a tissue. "I wish I had told him. I wish I had told him how much he meant to me."

Mercedes lightly touched Helen's shoulder. "I think every person here could say the same thing. He touched so many people with his kindness."

Helen sniffled and looked down at the blue-green carpet. "I've got to decide what to do with his house. I could use a fresh start."

Mercedes watched as the confident woman, who first approached them, now refused to meet their gaze. *Is she hiding something?*

Grant continued the conversation, oblivious to the change in demeanor. "Shady Springs is a great place to start over. If you need help moving or even if you decide to sell, here is a card with my number. We can get some church members to help move boxes or something."

Helen thanked him and excused herself. Before she made it to the door, Harold intercepted her. Mercedes couldn't help but notice the two made a handsome pair.

Grant interrupted her thoughts and pointed at two women standing by the exit. "Looks like my mom and Alice are ready to go."

"I told them I'd drive them home when they were ready. I guess I'll see you at home." She gave him a peck on the cheek and approached Carol and Alice.

"Do you want to stay longer?" she asked them.

"It's too creepy." Alice shook her head. "That man in the casket isn't my Chase. That's not how I want to remember him."

"Alice!" her mother admonished, looking slightly embarrassed. The funeral directors were listening to the conversation in earnest. "They did a good job presenting him. He looked very nice."

"Let's go," Alice headed toward the exit. "Can we stop at the diner and pick up a meal for Mark?" Alice held up her phone. "Mark sent a text saying he's starving."

"Sure," said Mercedes. "Go ahead and call it in so we can pick it up on the way."

She smiled as Alice called in a burger and key lime pie.

After they picked up his meal and arrived at the hospital, Mercedes parked in the lot. Alice stopped and stared at them as they got out of the car.

"You guys are coming in too?" she asked.

"I want to see how he's doing," Carol said.

"I'm just being nosy." Mercedes laughed.

"Whatever." Alice rolled her eyes. Mercedes exchanged an amused expression with Carol, and they linked arms behind Alice.

"Why do I feel you two are ganging up on me?" Alice called out behind her.

"Probably because we are," Mercedes snickered.

They followed Alice into Mark's hospital room. Cuts and bruises peppered his swollen face.

"It looks worse than it is." Mark smiled at them reassuringly.

"We're so glad you are okay, Mark." Carol sat in a chair in the corner of the room.

"Are you in much pain?" Mercedes said, surprised by his cheerfulness.

"Yes, but the medicine helps a lot. I'm just so glad I'm alive, you know?" He winked at Alice.

"Here's your food." Alice pushed the table over to his bed and placed his dinner on the table.

"Oh my gosh, thank you so much," he said as he dug into his burger.

Mercedes' jaw dropped as she watched him inhale it in three of the most enormous bites she'd ever seen. She looked at Alice in disbelief.

"Dude, seriously?" Alice shook her head in disgust.

"What? I told you I was starving." Mark popped open the plastic container of pie.

"How many bites will it take you to eat that?" Mercedes said dryly.

Unperturbed, Mark shrugged his shoulders and took a bite.

"He's just been in a car wreck. Give him a break, girls," Carol intervened.

"Thank you, Mrs. Carol," Mark beamed.

"Should've known my mom would take your side." Alice sighed.

"I can't help that I'm so charming," Mark said, his cheeks full of pie.

Even Mercedes couldn't stop from laughing at him.

Later at home, Mercedes warmed up a cup of tea after dropping Carol and Alice back at their house. She had spoken to Grant briefly before he left for the viewing, and he disclosed Alice's angel story. *I wonder if the man on my porch asking for gas money was an angel. I guess I'll never know.* Her husband seemed a little jealous that his sister had conversed with an angel. She, on the other hand, hoped this angel testing time was over. *Would she be more mindful of people around her and their needs? Yes, definitely.*

CHAPTER 16
Grant

Every day we live,
every moment in time is a gift.
—Grant

A few drops splashed on the windshield of Grant's truck. *Perfect,* he groaned inwardly, *Chase's funeral is today, I have no idea what I'm going to say and it's raining.* As if on cue, his phone rang in answer to his thoughts.

"Hey, Harold, I'm headed to the church."

"I was just calling to check in on you and see how you were holding up." Harold's voice rasped.

Grant felt a pang of guilt. He should be the one checking on his friend, not the other way around.

"Thanks, Harold. I'm all right. I'm having trouble finding the right words to say for the funeral. I want to do Chase justice, you know? I want to honor him."

"Chase was so proud of you, Grant. Whatever you say will be enough. Just pray about it, God will give you the words."

Grant wiped a tear from his eye. "I saw you talking with his niece, Helen, last night. Do you know her well?"

"Yes, I met her a few years ago. She's very nice."

"She mentioned Chase had left her his house, but didn't know what she was going to do with it."

"Do you think she might move here?" Harold's voice sounded a little brighter.

"She said she wanted a fresh start. So, possibly." Grant was surprised at his friend's interest. Harold had been a bachelor for so long. The senior ladies had been trying to nab him for years. He pulled into the church parking lot. "I'm at the church now, so I'm going to let you go."

"Maybe I should go by Chase's house and make sure it's okay—it would look bad on Shady Springs if vandals got in there."

"Good idea." Grant ended the call. *Harold is in his late sixties. There is a bit of an age difference between him and Helen, but it's not unheard of. Could Harold be interested in Helen romantically?* He shook Harold's love life out of his mind. No time for that now. He still had to figure out what to say for Chase's funeral. He only had a few hours before the funeral home directors arrived. He hurried into his office and shut the door, hoping for no more distractions for the day.

At precisely 11:00 a.m., Georgia and Pete from the funeral home were at the door, ready to bring in the casket and set up the flowers for the funeral. After letting them in, he returned to his office to change for the service. He finished tying his tie and opened the door to find himself face-to-face with Derek Rossi.

"Hi, Derek. Are you doing okay?" He hugged his friend.

"Yeah, I wanted to ask you if I could say a few words about Chase. He made such an impact on my life. I'd like to honor him." Derek looked at him hesitantly.

"Absolutely, that would be a great testament to his life." Grant smiled encouragingly.

"Great, just let me know when you want me to speak," Derek said.

"Will do. Do you mind checking with the ladies in the fellowship hall to see if there is enough food? They are preparing a meal for the family after the graveside service."

Grant headed toward the auditorium and arrived in the nick of time. Gladys stood hand on hip, the other hand waving a rose in the air. Georgia from the funeral home stood with arms crossed and lips tightly drawn.

"Gladys, I think the ladies in the fellowship hall need your guidance," he said, trying to distract her.

"Pastor Grant, you know flowers are my thing. I did the flowers for your wedding. I do the flowers for church. Chase was a dear friend. Please, let me do this," Gladys pleaded.

"You know what? It's fine. It's not worth getting upset about. She can redo them. I'll be in the foyer if you need anything." Georgia threw her hands up, smiled tightly, and walked away.

Grant watched as Gladys fussed around, moving the flowers in different directions. She seemed to be getting more distressed by the minute.

"I just can't get them the way I want. Chase deserves them to be perfect and they are not cooperating." She began to cry as she tried to stab a rose farther into an arrangement. Grant calmly rescued the rose and put his arm around her.

"The flowers look fine, Gladys. Chase wouldn't know the difference between the arrangements anyhow." Grant tried to soothe her.

"I know, I know. It's hard getting old and seeing your friends die one by one. You don't know what it's like. Wondering who will be next. Wondering if it will be me," she sobbed.

Grant just held her. *She's right. I don't know what it's like. How can I comfort her, Lord? Give me the words to say.*

"None of us know when it's our time, Gladys, people die young and old. Every day we live, every moment in time, is a gift. We treat it as such and know, when our time comes to an end, the Lord is ready for us to come home." Grant rubbed her back.

"Thank you, Pastor. I think maybe I just need to sit a minute and get myself together."

"Sit all you want. There are plenty of people around helping. You deserve a minute." He smiled.

She nodded and sat on the front row.

"Excuse me, Pastor, here is the slideshow and music for the service." Pete handed him a USB drive.

Grant made his way to the sound booth located in the back of the building. He breathed a sigh of relief to see his sound man sitting in the booth. *Sound person*, he corrected himself. Kinley was a technology guru, and she had made huge strides in keeping their church up-to-date. She started broadcasting their services on different social media platforms and even helped him start a podcast.

"Kinley, you've no idea how glad I am you are here. I've got the music and the slideshow for the service on this USB drive, praying it works on our computer here. You know how technology likes to fight us." Grant handed her the drive.

"No worries, Pastor. I got you. And there's still time to figure things out if it doesn't work." Kinley pushed her glasses up on her nose and plugged the drive into her computer.

"I'll bring you a schedule, so you'll know when to play things." Grant said.

"Already got one from the funeral director." She held up a piece of paper.

"Great. Derek is going to say something too. I think we'll fit him in after the obituary reading."

Kinley pulled a pencil from her hair and made a note on her copy. "Sounds good. Let me work on this, and I'll let you know if we are good to go."

"Awesome. Thank you." Grant turned to face the auditorium, trying to remember what else needed to be done before the service started. Sound. Flowers. Video. Food. Casket. He stopped for a moment. The directors had not brought the casket in. He stepped into the foyer, almost running into the pallbearers bringing in the dark cherry wood casket.

Good. Can't have the funeral without the casket. He could just imagine Chase laughing at not making it to his own funeral.

"Hey, you." Mercedes hugged his side and kissed him on the cheek. He hugged her back, pausing for a moment as he caught a whiff of her perfume. He said a silent thank you to God for the amazing woman He had gifted him.

"You look stressed. Is everything okay?" She patted his back.

"I think everything is coming together. I'm better now that you are here." He smiled.

"Is there anything I can do?"

"Gladys is having a tough time, if you want to check on her." He pointed to the older woman still sitting in the front row.

Mercedes gave him another kiss and made her way to Gladys. He watched as they exchanged a few words and Gladys stood and joined her, leaving for the kitchen.

Kinley came up beside him. "Everything is good to go. The slideshow and music uploaded fine, and we will be ready to start when it's time."

"Terrific, thanks," he said.

After the ceremony, Grant sat in his office with the door closed, relishing a few moments of solitude. The funeral service and graveside ceremony went without a hitch. Derek spoke about how Chase would visit him on Saturday mornings and pick him up on the church bus on Sundays. He reminisced about how Chase had mentored him and helped shape him into the man he is today. After Grant preached, three people raised their hands, indicating they had accepted Christ as their Savior.

I get so bogged down in the doing and the checklist. Lord, help me never lose sight of what is essential. Only what's done for You will last.

A knock came at his door, and a note shot underneath. He wiped away some tears and stood to answer it. Curious, he picked up the note. It was addressed to him. He took a letter opener from his desk to open it. The most irritating thing he found in life was a paper cut.

"Grant," Mercedes called through the door. "Are you in there?"

He put the note in his suit jacket for later and went to open the door.

"Yes, I just needed a minute to myself," he said.

His wife wrapped her arms around him and kissed him. "Take all the time you need. You've had a very long week."

"Seriously, guys? Save it for home, puh-lease," Alice complained, stepping through the doorway.

"What? I thought you weren't bothered by this now that you and Mark are a thing," Grant teased.

"I never said that. Chase's family is asking to see you at the dinner, Grant. So, stop all that and come on." She led them out the door.

"Let's go before they send someone else." Mercedes laughed and grabbed his hand, pulling him with her.

"Hey, did you see anyone else in the hallway just now?" Grant asked, thinking back to the note he'd received.

"Nope, why?" Mercedes asked.

"It's nothing," he said.

Chase's family and some of the congregation filled the fellowship hall. "How's the food? Can I get anyone anything?" He stopped at a table, taking special note of the person sitting on Harold's right side.

Helen Dimpsey beamed brightly at him. "Our family can't believe your congregation prepared all this food for us. We can't thank you enough."

Mercedes grabbed his arm. "Why don't you come sit over here, honey? I fixed you a plate."

"Thanks." Grant nodded at the table and joined his wife. He took a few bites of some fried chicken. "I didn't think I could eat anything, but I'm starving."

"There's plenty of food if you want more. I think Derek panicked and ordered some pizza," she laughed.

"People can take food home. It will be a blessing." He scanned the room and realized once again his friend was missing. Chase would have been in the kitchen, annoying all the ladies, going around the tables with the coffeepot and refilling people's cups. He felt a few tears fall down his cheek and dabbed at them with his napkin. No one seemed to notice his turmoil of emotions. They continued eating with hushed talking and laughter. *Get a grip, Grant. Reel it back in.* Emotionally drained and finished with his food, he threw his plate away and grabbed the coffeepot. He started to head out to the tables, but Derek stopped him.

"Why don't you let me get that?" Derek asked and took the pot from him. He gave him a knowing look and patted his shoulder.

Harold came and stood beside him. "It was a great service and graveside. Chase would have been pleased. You did good." He put his arm around him.

"Thanks." They stood silently until it was time to walk Helen and the rest of Chase's family out to their cars. Grant couldn't help but notice how Harold sidled up to Helen and how she looked back at him.

"Mercedes said you should go home and rest. They've almost got everything cleaned up," Alice said, coming up beside him.

"I think I'm going to take her up on that," Grant replied through a yawn.

"I know I give you a hard time most of the time, but I'm proud of you, big brother. I know this was a hard day. I love you." She gave him a hug, and his mind flashed back to right after their father had passed.

Alice sat on the steps to their house in her overalls and pigtails, crying. He didn't know if she understood their father was gone for good, or if she cried because everyone else cried.

"Why are you crying?" he asked.

"I lost my doll. What if she never comes back, just like Daddy? People keep apologizing for our loss, but lost things come back sometimes, don't they?" He later found her doll for her, and she hugged him tightly. "I love you, big brother. Don't you ever get lost."

"I love you too," Grant said, returning to the present. He hugged her back and waved goodbye to some of his members. The drive home was a blur. Throwing his suit jacket on the couch and the keys on the coffee table, he stumbled up the stairs and collapsed on his bed.

CHAPTER 17

Mercedes

I've made so many mistakes,
and God still forgives me.
—Mercedes

Mercedes came in later that evening, equally tired. Her poor husband had fallen asleep with the lights on and still in his suit pants and shirt. She turned off their bedroom light and pulled a throw blanket over her husband. After getting herself ready for bed, she snuggled under her comforter. This was her first funeral as a pastor's wife, and she hoped she had served their congregation well. *I don't know how my husband does this. I didn't do nearly as much as he did today, and I am wiped out.*

She closed her eyes and opened them to the smell of a fresh pot of coffee. A cloud of confusion crossed her mind. *What day is it?* Yesterday was the funeral. Today was Sunday, church again. A quick glance at her phone told her she'd better get out of bed and fuel herself with her morning elixir, or she would run late. Grant liked to arrive at church early, and she wanted to have some alone time with him before she had to share him with the rest of the congregation. She groaned, pushed herself out of bed, and wrapped herself in her fuzzy robe.

"Morning gorgeous." Her sweet husband kissed her forehead and handed her a cup of coffee. He had bacon and eggs cooking and was already dressed in a new shirt and tie.

She tried to say something coherent, but it emerged like a growl. She plopped at the kitchen table, closed her eyes, and downed the cup in three gulps.

"More, please," she croaked, handing her mug up.

"You might want to slow down with that." Grant laughed as he took the mug from her.

"Don't joke about my coffee," Mercedes said. She perked as he gave her the refilled mug.

"What are you preaching about this morning? Belinda is out today, so I am filling in on the piano." She slowed her pace down with this cup, savoring each sip.

"I'm preaching out of Psalms 103:8-10 on grace. The Lord has been speaking to me about His grace and how we can reflect that grace to others." Grant set a plate of food in front of her.

"You are too good for me, you know that? I feel like I should be making you breakfast," Mercedes said.

"I like getting up early, and I like cooking. It makes me happy to spoil you in the morning. You help me and encourage me in more ways than you realize." Grant joined her at the table with his plate.

"I don't think I do all that much, Grant. We work together on the different chores and projects around the house. I'm not sure if I contribute enough; I don't want to make it all about me," she said.

"You've turned this house into a home. I used to spend all my time at church because I didn't want to come home to an empty house. Now I can't wait to come home. Now I've got gardens and couch pillows." Grant stuffed a piece of bacon in his mouth.

"Gardens and couch pillows?" Mercedes burst out laughing. "I love you, Grant Ford."

"I love you too." He winked.

After they ate, Grant left for church, and she went back upstairs to get dressed.

Her phone pinged.

Forgot my suit jacket. Will you bring it with you?

Yes. Which one?

The one on the couch.

She replied yes and finished getting ready for church. Grant had gotten her a new boho-style maxi dress. She loved how comfortable the dress was. Some of her other dresses were feeling a little snug. Finally ready, she grabbed his jacket. An envelope addressed to her husband fell out of it.

She turned it over, noticing it still sealed, and stuck it back inside the pocket. *Wonder who it's from? I'll have to remember to ask Grant about it later.*

When Mercedes got to church, the song director pulled her aside to review the morning songs and schedule. She started filling in for their church pianist when she was out of town or sick. It felt good to have a role in the worship service again. As they were going over the last song, Grant interrupted them for his jacket.

"I set it over on the chair in the first row," Mercedes called out.

"Got it! Thanks," he said, sliding it on. "By the way, Sonja called me. She tried texting you. Stella has an ear infection. She wanted to know if you could step into the youth group with Derek this morning. I told her you would."

"No problem, I'll head on over there. Those girls can get a little wild sometimes." She pulled out her cell and saw the missed messages from Sonja.

Sorry, I missed your messages. On my way to youth. Let me know how Stella is doing. She texted back, then threw her phone into her purse.

When she reached the class, Derek settled everyone in their seats. Mercedes pulled up a chair beside one of the girls. She appreciated the updated space Sonja and Derek had created. Chalkboard signs with Bible verses adorned the freshly painted gray walls. The back wall became a focal wall of horizontal wooden planks. They had even procured a ping-pong table and fancy game system.

As Derek led the youth in their lesson, Mercedes remembered when she had first met him. It was not Derek's finest hour. In fact, he had tried to scare her away from Shady Springs. He thought she had known things that would have destroyed his marriage. However, he decided he wanted to be a better man and come clean with Grant and his wife. That scared, defeated man now stood with confidence and a care for others and the Lord. Bits from a Bible verse came to her mind. *He giveth more grace. God resists the proud but gives grace to the humble. Derek is a perfect example of that scripture. Then again, I suppose I am as well. I've made so many mistakes, and God still forgives me. He still blesses me. His grace really is amazing.*

"You are doing a great job with them." Mercedes helped him fold up some of the chairs at the end of the lesson.

"Thanks. I'm surprised how much I enjoy working with them. Most of the time, I feel like I'm learning more than they are," he said with a laugh.

"Mrs. Mercedes, they need you on the platform," one of the youth girls called through the door.

"Okay, coming. See you next door." She grabbed her stuff and sprinted to the auditorium.

"I've been looking all over for you," a voice called to her from behind.

Mercedes sighed as she recognized the voice. "Gladys, walk with me quick. I've got to play today."

"I just wanted you to know how much I appreciate you. I know all this pastor wife stuff is new for you, and I think you are doing wonderfully." Gladys threw her arms around her, throwing her off balance.

Shocked, Mercedes hugged her back, steadying herself on the brick walkway leading to the side of the church. "Wow, thank you, Gladys."

"Mercedes, it's time for the service to start." Grant motioned from the door to the auditorium.

"Coming," she said. *Lord, please be with the service today. Help every note I play bring honor and glory to You. Guide my hands and our hearts.* She silently prayed as the service began.

After the service, she met her husband in his office. "Ready for lunch?"

"Yes, I'm starving." He grabbed his keys. "Am I driving or you?"

"You drive. Your mom's pot roast sounds so good right now. Although I must admit a Sunday afternoon nap sounds rather tempting," Mercedes said.

"You had a busy morning. Youth group and then playing for the service. You played beautifully." He kissed her on the cheek as they walked out.

"Thanks. Derek is doing an amazing job with the youth. They respond to him so well. Oh, and Gladys said nice things to me today," she said with a laugh.

"It's always a brighter day when Gladys is being pleasant," Grant opened the door for her. "Alice said she's picking up Mark from the hospital, and they are stopping by for Sunday lunch."

"Yay! I'm surprised they are releasing him so soon," Mercedes said as she buckled her seat belt.

"No surprise to me after the wheelchair stunt he pulled. He can't stay still in one place without going crazy. I like the guy, but he's got energy like ants on steroids."

When they reached Carol's house, Alice and Mark were already inside.

"It's good to see you out of the hospital, Mark," Mercedes said, hugging him.

"It's good to be out! I was going insane in that place." Mark shook Grant's hand.

She caught a sideways wink from her husband behind Mark's back and grinned, shaking her head.

"And y'all know I need a good home-cooked meal after all that hospital food," Mark continued.

"Well, let's go sit at the table since we are all here." Carol gestured to the kitchen with a smile. They slowly followed a limping Mark through the small kitchen into the dining room.

"Sorry, I guess I should have gone in last," he called over his shoulder.

They piled around the table and began to eat and talk.

"Grant, I was wondering if you would mind if I cut the work in your attic short? There's not much left up there. Mark needs my help opening the shop while he is recovering. He's also gotten behind cataloging items. Would you be angry with me?" Alice shoved a bite of mashed potatoes in her mouth.

"Gee, I don't know. I was counting on you to get that done. I can't believe you would just quit on me like that," Grant said.

Mercedes rolled her eyes and hit her husband on the arm. "He's joking. Of course, you can help Mark instead. Grant's just upset because now he has to do it."

"Who said anything about me doing it? Didn't you say you wanted more things to do around the house?" Grant asked incredulously.

"You know that was not what I meant. I'm still too traumatized to go back up there because of Martin Pitrones." Mercedes shook her dinner roll at him, laughing.

"I don't think we will ever see him again in this town. The sheriff let him know he wasn't welcome," Grant said.

"Do you think the testing is over? That the angels are finally done with us?" Alice asked.

"I think so. Although, every time I see someone with a need, I will look closer at them." Grant unbuttoned his suit jacket. "I think I ate too much. My jacket is feeling snug."

"That's from being married," his mom said. "Everyone gains weight after they get married."

Grant removed his jacket, and the note fell on the floor.

"I saw that earlier today, and I forgot to ask you about it," Mercedes said as she scooped it from the floor and handed it to her husband.

"Oh yeah, someone slipped it under my office door yesterday. I never got around to opening it. I figured it was a thank you note or something from one of Chase's family members." He took a butter knife from the table and slit the envelope open.

He carefully opened the letter and read the contents out loud.

Dear Pastor Grant,

You and your family have shown sufficient grace to others. Keep your eyes open for the poor and learn from them. They are with you always. Count your blessings.

Grace and peace until the next forty years.

XX

"XX? What does that mean?" Mercedes asked.

"That's how they signed it. Here, take a look." Grant handed her the note.

Mark smacked the table loudly, causing everyone to jump. "The camera!" he yelled.

Everyone looked at him in confusion.

"Are you feeling all right?" Alice asked in concern.

"Don't you remember the camera? I loaned one of them a camera from the shop, and the officer took it as evidence! What if we caught evidence of an angel on the camera?" Mark said.

"I forgot about that! Grant, can you use your pastor clout with Lydia to see if we can get a look at the photos?" Alice asked.

"Pastor clout? Seriously?" Grant shook his head.

"Don't let it go to your head, but you have a little more sway being the pastor," Mercedes said.

"Fine, I'll text her now and see what she says. I don't know if she is working today." Grant pulled out his phone.

"What are we going to do about the next pastor?" Mercedes asked.

"What do you mean?" Grant said.

"Are you going to leave a cryptic message for him in the attic?" Alice asked.

"No, definitely not. I don't know. I could write a letter to him or maybe a journal with what events transpired with Martin and our stories," Grant plopped a mountain of potatoes on his plate and began to smother them in brown gravy.

"I like the journal idea," Mark said. "Much easier to deal with than figuring out what technology will still be in play forty years from now."

"That's true. I'm sure Martin never imagined how far technology would come since that answering machine." Grant's phone pinged. "Lydia's not in the office today, but she said we could come by tomorrow to look at the pictures. She said she has an interesting story for us."

"Can we go after I get off work? I don't want to miss possible angel pictures," Mercedes said.

"Will you pick me up? I don't want to miss it either," Mark asked Alice.

"I suppose I can. You know, you are asking an awful lot of me. This is turning out to be a very high-maintenance relationship," Alice said.

"I know. I promise I'll make it up to you." Mark touched his heart in earnest.

"There is a table full of witnesses; don't even think about backing out of it." She pointed at him with her fork.

"Is your sister always this scary?" Mark asked Grant.

"Yes. Pretty much." Grant nodded matter-of-factly and shoved a spoonful of mashed potatoes in his mouth.

"Good to know. Thanks." Mark laughed.

CHAPTER 18

Alice

I don't think I'll ever get over how God uses impossible situations
to bring people to Him.
—Grant

The sun shone with a golden hue by the time Alice turned down the dirt road leading to Mark's house. Mark sat on his front porch and began to hobble down the steps as she pulled in front of his home.

"Were you tired of being indoors?" She opened the car door for him.

"Kind of. My mom kicked me out of the house." He grinned.

"What? Why?" She closed his door and walked to the driver's side.

"She said I drove her crazy by changing the channels and talking too much." He shrugged his shoulders as she pulled out of the driveway.

"Mark," she sighed.

"I know, I have a lot of energy. It's good when I have an outlet but not so good when I'm confined." He gave her a small smile.

She couldn't help but smile at him in return. "Let's go see if we caught angels on camera."

"Anybody come into the shop today?" Mark asked.

"Two older ladies came in and bought some jewelry. They were attending an afternoon tea and wanted some bling." She laughed.

"Bling?" Mark repeated.

"I tried not to laugh in the store because that's the word they used. They came in and said, 'We're looking for some bling.' Also, a younger man came in and purchased a painting. He rented his first apartment, and his mother plans to visit. He thought some decorations would impress her."

"What painting did he get?" Mark tapped his fingers on his armrest.

"At first, he decided on those ugly flower paintings, but I talked him out of them. I told him if he were looking at this art-work on his wall daily, he needed to pick something he wouldn't get tired of. He finally settled on those two abstract paintings with white, orange, and gold circles."

"That's one of the things I love about the shop—hearing other people's stories and being able to contribute something to that story." Mark continued to tap.

"It's fun. I can see why you like it. I also cataloged the match-books and glass doorknobs and uploaded them to the website.

There is so much randomness in your store." She shook her head and laughed.

"I know, I think that's why it appeals to me. Lots of little things to keep my attention."

Tap. Tip, tip. Tap. Tip, tap. Mark began a new rhythmic pattern with his fingers. Unable to ignore it any longer, she grabbed Mark's hand with her right hand as she continued to steer with her left hand.

"Sorry." Mark colored slightly and looked out the window.

"It's okay." Alice squeezed his hand and gave him a reassuring smile.

"Although, wasn't a bad way to get you to hold hands with me."

She glanced over at him in time for him to wink at her. "Mark!" She wanted to drop his hand and hit him, but she liked the feel of his strong hand in hers. "Looks like Grant and Mercedes aren't here yet. Let's wait in the car till they get here." Alice reluctantly let go of his hand as she pulled into a parking space.

"Sounds good to me. Police stations don't hold my best memories." Mark unbuckled his seat belt and leaned back against the headrest.

"How many times were you arrested or brought in or whatever?"

"Let's see. . . There was the time I borrowed the car with Derek and my brother, the time I got drunk and rode my horse into the dollar store, two fights that I got into at a bar out where

I used to work. What can I say? I've done a lot of stupid stuff. Does that give you second thoughts about being with me?"

"Absolutely not, Mark. I've done plenty of things I'm not proud of, maybe not to the extent of yours. But, your bar fighting days are over, right?"

"For sure. Funny how none of that really appeals to me anymore."

"What does appeal to you?" Alice looked down at her nails. Mark lifted her chin, causing her eyes to meet his. She felt heat rise to her cheeks as he pushed a loose strand of her hair behind her ear.

"If you don't know by now, I must be doing something wrong."

Before she could respond, Grant rapped on Mark's window. She felt relief and regret wash over her at the break of the intimate moment. She noticed Mercedes side-eyeing her with a big grin as she exited the vehicle. She held Mercedes' arm and let Grant and Mark get a head start in front of them.

"Cut it out," she whispered.

"Do you two need a chaperone?" Mercedes whispered back teasingly.

"No, we don't need a chaperone," Alice muttered. "Please, don't embarrass me."

Mercedes put her arm around her. "Sorry, I didn't mean to. I won't say anything more."

"No more looks?" Alice added.

"No more looks." Mercedes opened the door to the station as Lydia met them at the counter.

"Great, you are all here. Come on back, and let's talk," Lydia said. She grabbed a file folder and led them to an interrogation room.

"This is the same room we were in last time with M.P.," Mercedes whispered to them. They situated themselves around an empty table with a tape recorder sitting in the middle.

"Before I show you these pictures, I want to go back to the day when Mark here had his accident," Lydia said. "As you know, we got an anonymous tip about the accident before Grant called. We have that call recorded here." Lydia pressed play on the recording. Alice almost fell out of her chair.

"That's him! That's the man—or angel—I talked to. I'm sure of it!" she said excitedly.

"If he hadn't called when he did, the paramedics said you might not have made it," Lydia said.

"I heard him say my name, but all I could see was his eyes and light. It could have been the morning sun blinding me." Mark said.

"Or, maybe an angel," Alice interjected.

"Here are the pictures we got off the camera. There weren't very many," Lydia passed the folder to Grant. He opened the folder and pulled out some photos.

"What is it? Can you see them in the photographs?" Alice took a breath, trying to be patient with her brother.

He thumbed through the first few. "These are of us." He spread them on the table. There was a photo of Grant outside the donut shop, a photo of Alice at church, and Mercedes on her porch talking to the man who ran out of gas.

"It's a little creepy. Like angel stalkers?" Mark said.

"The Bible says there are angels who guard us. So think about how they are around us everywhere we go to help us." Alice picked up the picture of her and studied it.

"To help us, not take pictures of us," Mercedes clarified.

"I must admit, I was alarmed when I saw those," Lydia said. "Especially since we never could find that man in the cabin."

The last photo was a failed attempt at a selfie. The men had only gotten the top parts of their faces with a big blue sky in the background. At first glance, it looked like a typical picture with the red-eye feature off. Alice looked closer; those weren't red dots in their eyes from the camera's glare. Flames danced in their eyes.

"Take a closer look at their eyes. That is weird." She slid the photo to Mark.

"Really weird," Mark said.

"We had the lab techs look at it, and they said it could be a reflection. They didn't know what to make of it." Lydia took the photos from them and put them back into the folder.

"Well, I'm a little disappointed. I thought we might have something here. Real evidence that people could say, yes, you had an angel visit you," Mark said.

"I understand your disappointment, but I had another reason I wanted you to come in today," Lydia said.

"What other reason?" Grant asked.

"Hang on, I want to introduce you to someone." Lydia left the room.

"Does anybody have any idea what's going on?" Mark said. "Cops make me nervous, especially when they say they have another motive."

"No clue," said Mercedes.

Lydia entered the room with a pretty, caramel-complexioned young woman. "Everyone, this is Jenny. She has started covering for me as dispatcher."

"Hi, I wanted to meet you all because I handled your call on Thursday." Jenny looked down and fiddled with her hands.

"Oh, wow. Thank you!" Mark said.

"It's you I need to thank, or maybe you?" She looked at Mark and then Grant.

"I'm not sure why you need to thank me. I didn't do anything." Grant smiled.

"But you did. When you talked to Mark until the ambulance arrived, I was still on the line," she said.

"I'm sorry. I'm still not following you," Grant replied.

"I went to church with my boyfriend last week, and the service left me with a lot of questions about eternity. I had been praying for God to show me how I could have certainty in knowing I was going to Heaven. When I heard you pray to

Jesus to save you, I decided to do that too." Jenny shrugged and smiled.

"Well, how about that! Congratulations!" Mark exclaimed.

"That's amazing. I don't think I'll ever get over how God uses impossible situations to bring people to Him," Grant said.

CHAPTER 19

Mercedes

Moments like this last forever.
—Mercedes

"**S**o, I guess that is it, then?" Mercedes said. She smoothed her hair from her face as she pushed the hope chest toward the opening in the attic floor.

"What?" Alice grabbed the chest from where she stood on the step ladder below.

"The end of our mystery messages and angelic visitors. Things will finally start to quiet down." Mercedes held her end while Alice moved backward down the ladder.

"I certainly hope so. Thank you for giving me this hope chest. I've always wanted one."

"My grandpa made mine. He made it extra big because he said I needed a lot of hope. He thought he was a comedian," she said. "Do you know what you are going to put in it?" Mercedes huffed as they finally made it down the ladder, chest intact.

"I've got a few things from my grandmother—some glass she collected from the Great Depression and a quilt." They set the chest down and took a breather.

"Well, now we just have to get it down the staircase." Mercedes laughed. "Maybe we should wait for Grant to come home."

"Where is he? Isn't he usually home by now?" Alice asked.

Mercedes shrugged. "I think he had a stop to make."

"Was there anything else you wanted up there?" Mercedes asked.

"If you don't want that quilt, I'd like it. I thought it was pretty," Alice said.

Mercedes turned toward the ladder. "Sure, I'll go back and get it."

"You don't have to go back and get it now. It can wait," Alice said.

Mercedes took a few steps up the ladder and shook her head. "No, it can't. I want to get this attic cleaned out."

"You're not mad at me for backing out?" Alice called out worriedly.

"Don't be silly. There's not that much left to do anyway." She surveyed the few piles left and beelined for the quilt. Pursing her lips in thought, she made a mental note to add *finish the attic* to Grant's honey-do list.

She had a definite ulterior motive for finishing the attic. A positive sign on a pregnancy stick indicated the attic would be off-limits to her after a few months. She wanted one project checked off her to-do list before she couldn't do much else.

Grant had no idea he would soon be a daddy. She had wanted to tell him earlier, but too much was going on. She had searched for different ways to tell your husband you're pregnant while she was at work and found the perfect thing. She couldn't wait for it to arrive and to give it to her husband.

Hugging the quilt, she carefully backed down the ladder.

"Alice, you still there?" she called over her shoulder. She took another step down the ladder and jolted. A piece of the quilt had gotten stuck in the mechanics of the ladder. She reached up to pull it off. The ladder began to wobble. *No. Please, Lord, don't let me fall. Don't let anything happen to this baby.*

She tried to steady the ladder and cried out for help.

Strong arms came around her. "I got you. Take two more steps down."

"Grant," she sighed in relief. "Thank God."

"Why are you on the ladder by yourself? I know we are on a stretch with zero accidents in the homeplace, but still. . ." She could hear the amusement in his voice. After one month of marriage, Grant posted a sign on their refrigerator with the number of accidents in the workplace. He thought she wouldn't be so accident-prone if she had a safety goal. He wouldn't be too happy if he knew she was up there alone and pregnant. *The attic project is going to have to wait. Nothing is worth going through a scare like that again.*

"Where's Alice?" She hugged him tight.

"Where do you think?" He rolled his eyes. "I brought Mark by after his physical therapy, and they are being all lovey-dovey."

"We better get downstairs before they get too lovey-dovey," she said, grabbing his arm.

"Mercedes, there's a package for you," Alice called out as they entered the living room. Mark sat on a recliner, and Alice sat in a chair beside him.

"What's that? Did you order something?" Grant picked it up and read the label. "Babies World?"

Heat rose from her neck to the top of her head. This was not going as planned. She snatched it from her husband.

"Oh yes, I think I got this for baby Stella. I'll go stick it upstairs."

"Wait, I want to see what you got her. I love baby girl clothes. They are so cute! Just like doll clothes!" Alice exclaimed.

"Oh, it's not that cute." Mercedes shook her head. "I can't even remember why I bought it. It's not that exciting."

"Mercedes, you always find the cutest gifts; quit being modest," Alice said.

"Alice, I—" She continued to shake her head in protest.

"What's the big deal, hon? Just show her the gift," Grant prodded.

If looks could kill and you weren't my baby daddy right now, Grant Ford. She felt her temper rise.

"Here then, Grant. You open it and show her." She smiled, shoved the package at him, and sat on the couch, making him the center of attention.

"Seriously?" he asked her incredulously. "I don't understand why you are making such a fuss."

He opened the plastic package and pulled out the baby onesie.

"Daddy's new riding buddy." He held it up for everyone to see. "That's cool. I don't think Derek rides motorcycles."

"That's because it's not for Derek and Sonja," Mercedes said, crossing her arms in front of her.

"Well, who's it for then? Nobody else in the church is pregnant right now." Grant looked at her in confusion.

She gave him a pointed look. "What? It's for us? That's sweet. I get it now. You saw it and bought it, thinking ahead for when we have a baby, and didn't want to be embarrassed."

"Sweetheart," she sighed. "I bought it for now because you will have a new riding buddy in approximately nine months."

"Oh, my stars!" Alice screamed and jumped up and down. "I can't believe it. I'm going to be an aunt!"

Grant stared at Mercedes, frozen.

She walked to him and took the onesie from him. "Do you need to sit down?"

"Is this a joke? Am I going to be a dad?" He finally spoke.

"Yes. You are going to be a dad. This is not a joke. I'm sorry. I planned to tell you privately, but you kept pushing me. Anyway, I couldn't keep it a secret any longer. Are you happy?" She hesitated. Maybe she'd made the wrong move.

"Happy? I'm ecstatic! This is amazing. This is the best news ever. I can't believe we're having a baby." Grant pulled her in and hugged her. She felt wetness on her cheeks and realized she was crying.

"Wait. Why are you crying?" Grant pulled away and studied her intently.

"I'm just so happy. Moments like this last forever. I love you so much."

"When? When am I going to meet my baby niece or nephew?" Alice wrapped her arms around both of them, jumping with glee.

"February or March. I haven't been to the doctor yet," Mercedes said.

"Here, sit down a minute. Everyone, calm down and have a seat," Grant said, leading her to the couch. He sat on one side, and Alice sat on the other.

"Congratulations," Mark said. "I wish I could jump up and down, but Alice jumped around enough for everyone."

Alice stuck her tongue out at him.

CHAPTER 20

Alice

I guess we make a pretty good team.
—Mark

Alice stared at her ceiling, thinking about everything that had transpired over the last few days. She couldn't believe she was going to be an aunt. How could she miss her sister-in-law being pregnant and having the baby? She didn't want to go back to college and miss everything. *Mom would have a conniption if I dropped out of college with only one year left.* She pulled out her cell phone and looked at what classes she had left to take. A rap came at her door, and her mom peeked her head in.

"Are you still awake?" her mother asked.

"Wide." She sighed. "There's so much to think about with Mercedes having a baby, Mark and his shop, and then me going back to college in a month. I wish I had gone to a closer college.

Is it crazy to try to transfer in my last year?" Alice looked at her mom.

"Scootch over," her mom said. Alice moved to the side so her mom could lie beside her.

"I don't think it's crazy. But before you decide, examine all the options. Online courses or a transfer might work. You might have to buck up and do the last year there. Let's look at it tomorrow. I miss you and selfishly would like you back home for a while before you decide to leave me and get married." Her mom snuggled beside her. "Mark isn't pressuring you to drop out, is he?"

"What? No, we aren't that serious yet. We are both still trying to figure out what we want in life. I would like to see how solid his beliefs and relationship with the Lord are before we start getting too serious. I do think I'm falling in love with him, Mom. I really do." Alice laid her head on her mother's shoulder.

"I think it's wise of you to let Mark find his new self in the Lord. Make sure to give him some grace. Finding your identity in Christ has beautiful results, but it can be a messy process. How are you dealing with Chase's death?" Carol asked.

"You know, I almost took a summer job in Magnolia, but something told me to come home. I would have been devastated if I had been away when he died. I'm going to miss him so much. Grant said his niece is considering moving to town and has a college-age daughter." She ran her finger over the stitching on her comforter.

"I met his niece at the funeral. Helen's her name, I think. She seemed like a nice lady," Carol said. They lay there in silence until Carol sighed and reluctantly pushed herself off the bed. "I better get to bed—early morning tomorrow."

Her mother kissed her forehead.

Are you ever too old to enjoy comfort from your mother? She hoped not. "Good night, Mom."

The following day, she made her way again to Priceless Junk. Today, she hoped to tackle some of the kitchen items. Mark had asked her to catalog and list some antique stoneware crocks and jugs on the website. He wanted to focus their attention on some of the higher-priced items in the store.

She had just finished photographing them when a tall woman came in.

"Can I help you?" she asked.

"Yes, I've got some boxes of items here that I'd like to get rid of." The woman wore classy linen shorts and a blouse.

"Do you want to sell or consign?" Alice asked. Mark had told her he didn't want to consign with people and didn't want to track other people's sales.

"I want to sell. I've got some basketball cards, vintage suits, and perhaps a few other items." The woman looked at her surroundings with interest. "You have quite the array of things here."

"Thank you. My friend actually owns the store. If you leave your name and number, I will have him call you." Alice took a notepad and pen off the counter.

"Helen Dimpsey, 887-555-3432. He can reach me any time after five. I'm leaving today, but I will be back next weekend. There's no rush." Helen started to push open the door.

"Would you happen to be Chase's niece, Helen?" Alice asked.

"That would be me." Helen blinked in surprise. "I guess this is a small town."

"The smallest." Alice laughed. "My mother told me she met you. We went to church with Chase. He was a special friend to our family."

"He was special. My biggest regret is that I didn't keep in touch with him better." Helen's shoulder slumped.

"Are you going to be moving here or selling the house?" Alice asked.

"I'm going to move here." Helen's shoulders squared back, and she jutted her chin out. "I think this town is just what I need. Time for a break from big city life."

"I can understand that. I about have a panic attack every time I drive through Little Rock," Alice said.

"Little Rock is nothing compared to driving through Dallas. I worry every time my daughter drives home from college," Helen said.

"Did she make it here for the funeral?" Alice said.

"She did, but she had to drive back the next day so she wouldn't miss her class on Monday."

"Maybe I'll meet her sometime when she visits you here. I go to SAU in Magnolia."

"I'd love for you to meet her. Oh dear, I never even got your name." Helen looked a little embarrassed.

"My name is Alice Ford. It's nice to meet you officially. I'll make sure my friend gets your message." Alice waved the paper as Helen thanked her and headed out the door. She spent the rest of the day cataloging and mailing orders from the online store. After a glance at today's online sales, Alice's jaw dropped. Grabbing her phone, she tapped Mark's name.

"Mark, guess what?"

"Well, hello to you too," he said, laughing.

"Hello, hello, guess what?" she said impatiently.

"Hmm...well. . .wait. . .no. . .that's probably not it," Mark drawled out every word.

She bit her lip, trying to be patient. Nope. She couldn't take it.

"I posted those jugs, and two of them sold. Mark! Two jugs! That's twelve hundred dollars!" she squealed into the phone.

"Ouch, my ear," Mark joked.

"I thought you would be excited."

"I am, truly I am. That's great."

"Also, a lady said she had some items to sell. Turns out she is Chase's niece and is planning to move here."

"Oh, cool. Did you get her name and number?"

"Yep. Sure did!"

"Hey, not bad. Good job!" he said.

"It was your idea."

"Yeah, but you are the one who did it. I guess we make a pretty good team." There was a softness in his voice that melted her heart every time.

"Looks like it," she said.

"Let's write this successful operation down now so we'll remember for later. First, I give the order, I mean directions, then you do what I say."

"Oh. You think that's how it's going to go?" Alice said, shaking her head.

"How else is it supposed to go?" Mark asked, laughing.

"Oh, you are about to learn, Mark. You are about to learn." Alice laughed, content with a joy and happiness she had never known.

EPILOGUE

Be not forgetful to entertain strangers:
for thereby some have entertained angels unawares.
—Hebrews 13:2 (KJV)

"**D**o you think Shady Springs will keep to the right course?" Mikey cast a side glance at his friend as they relaxed on a yellow bench. A small wren resting on a bus stop sign tilted his head toward them, eavesdropping on their conversation.

"I think they will. God only knows." Gabe shrugged. "Of course, I thought Atlantis people had it together, and we all know how that turned out." He leaned back against the bench, stretched his legs, and wiggled his toes through the hole in his shoe.

"Excuse me, sir. Sorry to interrupt." A mop of red curls and the beginning of pubescent acne perched on the seat of a ten-speed.

Gabe sat up. "What can we do for you?"

"I'm on my way home from the store. I just bought some new tennis shoes. Something told me to stop and give this to you." He shoved a white plastic bag toward them. "It's my old shoes. They are still in pretty good shape. I don't know if they'll fit."

Mikey took the bag from the boy and handed it to Gabe. "Thank you. I'm sure they will fit one of us." Gabe pulled the pair of shoes out and whistled.

"Sorry, Mikey, these are mine." He admired the shoes as he slipped them onto his feet. "Thank you, son."

A look of relief passed on the boy's face, and he grinned broadly. "You're welcome!"

"That Daniel has overcome a lot. God's going to do great things through him." Mikey nodded toward the boy as he rode away.

"I hope there are others like him where we are going. Speaking of which, where is our next assignment?" Gabe asked. Mikey handed him the bus tickets. "Staying in the South! Nice! I hope that barbecue place is still open. They had the best brisket." He patted his belly.

The wren took flight as the screeching of brakes interrupted their conversation. They stood to get on the bus, the only two in line. As usual, the people on the bus avoided eye contact with the scraggly pair. No one ever wanted to sit by them. An uneasiness washed over Mikey as he watched Shady Springs disappear from view. He sent a silent prayer to his Creator. Martin Pitrones still lurked about. Something was in the wind.

"Lord, I know there are tough times ahead for these people. Give them strength for what is headed their way."

Reflection Questions

1. What are ways Christians can show grace to others?

2. Have you ever had an angelic experience?

3. What angelic encounters are mentioned in the Bible?

4. Mark thought a Christian life might be boring. How would you witness to someone who thought that way?

5. Mark thought he was unworthy of God's goodness. Can you think of any Bible characters who struggled with this?

Acknowledgements

Thank you to my husband and children for giving me grace when it comes to book writing and all of the things that go with that!

Thank you to my author friend Rachel Miller for your wisdom and encouragement in finishing this project.

Special thanks to Karen Weido and Kay Smith for your honest feedback and support!

About the Author

Chrystal Gilkey is an author, speaker, and Bible study teacher. A Texas girl born and raised, she now resides in Arkansas with her husband, three children, and two spoiled pets. Chrystal writes to encourage and strengthen people's faith in God. She enjoys playing the piano and gardening. One day she dreams of owning a mini-pig.

Connect with her at chrystaljgilkey.com or find her on Tik-Tok, Facebook, Twitter, Instagram, and LinkedIn @chrystaljgilkey

Other Books

Every cloud has a silver lining . . . right? Unexpectedly out of a job, Meteorologist Mercedes Lewis responds to an intriguing email about a strange weather anomaly in Shady Springs. Carrying the burden of past hurts and an uncertain future, she heads to the small town hoping to uncover a story that will get her career—and her life—back on track. Pastor Grant Ford's ministry hangs in the balance—on a cloud. Literally. The people of Shady Springs have long believed the unique cloud that has hovered over the area for more than a century is a symbol of God's approval of their beloved town. But as the cloud diminishes, so does their faith in Grant's leadership. While Grant tries desperately to hold his church family together, Mercedes struggles with the decision to allow God to take control of her life.

Join Grant and Mercedes on a journey of faith as they uncover the past and search for the truth about God's plan for the future of Shady Springs and for themselves.

https://mybook.to/pj0MXB

Even the darkest shadows can cast hope.

After two miscarriages and desperate pleading with the Lord, Sonja Rossi thinks her prayers have been answered. She finds a baby on the banks of Shady Springs Lake and persuades her husband to take part in a plan to keep the child. She confides her delicate predicament to her close friend, Mercedes Lewis, but murder threatens to rock her cradle of hope.

Mercedes Lewis should be living her best life. She started a new job and is planning her wedding. Her preparations are shaken when her first love, Garrett King, arrives in Shady Springs and strangely pretends they've never met. His wife has also confided a secret of her own.

Can Mercedes keep up with all the pretense or will harboring Shady Springs' secrets sever her from those she loves the most?

https://mybook.to/DyHqrh

It's one of the hardest things to experience and speak about...

If you've experienced church hurt, you are not alone. Satan uses church hurt as a means to wound and disable Christians from furthering God's message of love and hope. However, there can be healing and restoration with the Lord. There can be forgiveness and peace. Author and speaker Chrystal Gilkey provides Biblical insight for reconciliation and spiritual healing.

Perfect for Bible Study Groups or individual study.

https://mybook.to/Su0zQo